Apples from the Garden of Eden

ROCCO SCIBETTA

ISBN 978-1-955156-08-0 (paperback)
ISBN 978-1-955156-07-3 (digital)

Rushmore Press LLC
1 800 460 9188
www.rushmorepress.com

Printed in the United States of America

PART I

Morning Becomes Alexis

It is autumn in the city, not deep autumn like the kind you see pictured on sympathy cards with curled dried leaves and swirling wind, but pleasant autumn—sunny and brisk with folks projecting happy faces in anticipation of the holiday season.

From the view of a moving bus window, one might think the local pageantry appears as an unfolding ribbon loop of coats and sweaters forming grids throughout the city. A visual artist the likes of a Mondrian or a Marlow Moss might perceive the procession as a rotary typewriter ribbon—twisting narrow bands of cloth with specially finished edges, recycling from one end of the spool to the other around and around back and forth, disappearing and appearing again, creating spaces and lines. A writer might be inspired to perceive the blue-black footprint residual shadow marks underfoot, marking the pavement. Each surviving mark generates a unique brand of alternative grapheme. Collectively, they become one: human letters and hashtags littering the avenue with excessive information.

The busy sidewalks are filling up with folks adorned in colors of the season. Commuters blend against the brick and mortar of brownstone buildings, reminding everyone that festivity and asphalt fashion make the season fun. Freshly painted enamel railings of black and gray become a wash of watercolor splashing down the street. All this orchestration becomes a blur from the window of the Main Street bus, without one tree to clutter the view.

Storeowners are staging their window displays. The last distractions of summer are falling off in pieces. A sundried billboard blocking the autumn sky features two young people running along a beach; their summer tans now sun faded and weather beaten, exposing the cracking poster marine board underneath. This landmark-avenue marquee soon to be replaced, however, by a digital photo image of a huge moving cornucopia of autumnal fruits and goodies cascading from a horn of plenty. It is an advertisement promoting a local farm. This is a city after all, not near a beach and not near a farm; nevertheless, the business of billboards is to transform us. Advertising subtlety suggests to the viewer that where they are is not where they need to be. That might be one reason why they project an image that is always of a place somewhere other than where you are—that unattainable, fantastic moment that always leaves you yearning.

It was Eighth Street and Broadway. A gentle gathering of clouds united themselves in front of the already-too-bright sun for this time of year, causing a flicker of silver lining to catch the eye of one Alexis Barrette who was contemplating downy formations from the window of the eight fifteen main.

Lexis, as her friends would call her, was an ordinary, nondescript, aging teenager with a pretty name. Hazing schoolmates at Belmont High School signed in her yearbook ("the girl most likely to write an encyclopedia on animal origins of property and nation" or something similar.) Moreover, she once aspired to become a curator for the comparative Museum of Comparative Zoology at Harvard. For the time being, however—lying lofty dreams aside—she is completing her studies in library science where her lust for research is serving her well. Her interest for data fills up her days with exciting day trips and visits to places outside her normal realm of trendy boutique coffeehouses and wall-to-wall carpeted study halls with Deco couches.

Gone are the hard, no-nonsense old oak library chairs of yesteryear. Clumsy constructs of modest and plain design, complete with spindle backs and carved buttock pine seats, were matched with scholarly oak tables and a reading lamp. The conspicuous high-tech era brought with it plush, comfortable lounge chairs and laptops of all kinds, transforming the dimmest trendy coffee bar or fast-food establishment into an internet cafe.

Gone also is the "shush!" and etiquette rule. Students are comfortable chatting, snacking, or lounging, so long as it is not too interruptive with fellow students. Flashing blinks and twinkles follow suit, producing bizarre split-second twinkling LED screens and cell phone beeps. Even Darwin in his solitary study would have been slow to suspect that the modern scholar would one day evolve into a social creature fraternizing through a social network that could deliver the exchange of ideas from all over the world in a few seconds. Study halls have become moveable feasts where friends could "hook up" in just a few clicks.

Lexis was a loyal friend. Her studies kept her from actively joining clubs or mingling with social groups, but she stayed close with the acquaintances she met along the way. Even as time brings changes to a young girl's life, Lexis was able to stay in touch with the old gang through the magic of social media.

Ah, thank goodness for social media, she thought to herself, finishing off the final clicks to a message on her smart phone before closing out to resume a last-ditch daydream before she reaches her destination.

The many times Lexis has traveled this venue enabled her to see the same stores and even the same faces; some have become so familiar to her that even though they have never met formally, people say hello in passing, just out of plain propinquity. Lexis became aware of herself saying hello to strangers all morning, keyed up and inwardly excited. Today is a special day.

Today, Lexis is en route to attend a lecture that she has been waiting for three weeks to attend. This afternoon at one o'clock, Sampson Hall is having Dr. Felix X. Cole discusses his new book. Lexis has been a follower of Dr. Cole's theories since high school and collected every book he has ever written since she discovered he was writing them. I suppose you could say that Lexis thought of Professor Cole as her subliminal soul mate. Cole, on the other hand, did not know Lexis existed, and neither would he care. Unbeknownst to Lexis, Prof. Felix. X. Cole was probably one of the most unimpassioned, empty-suited hacks that this planet is capable of turning out. Besides his ornery indifference to everything human, he is losing his marbles faster than the new kid in the schoolyard and is about to go clinically insane.

Hartman University—considered by many to be a leading institution in psychology promoting a better understanding of person and beast. "Hartman U," as is abbreviated on campus, has become a cornerstone in Lexis's life over the last two years. Lately, she has built her life around the campus. Being an only child and somewhat sheltered, Lexis has a somewhat myopic view of the outside world. Her interest in zoology and folklore studies enabled her to examine lifestyles and exotic cultures without having to travel much or to touch anything, which works out fine, as she has a genuine dislike for leaving her comfort zone and a wicked phobia about touching things without prior knowledge about them.

Today, young Lexis will have the opportunity to have her soul mate/mentor sign a copy of his book for her. Besides, she can confess to him at last, face to face, how moved she is by his thoughts and how his dedicated research had changed her life.

Comfortably relaxing now, Lexis turns her head to the window of the Main Street bus 10 looking out, watching the street signs fall in nickelodeon sequence. She is clutching a fresh new edition of Felix X. Cole's new magnum opus—*Lectures on the Traditional Mores and the Extinction of Marriage.*

Morning Has Broken

The sun had already been up for hours, but one would never know from the Havisham gloom that envelopes Felix X. Cole in his cryptic bedroom. An empty ashtray, a half-eaten donut, and some milk in glass are stationary on a small table. Carefully folded pants, a dress shirt, and tie, along with a pair of socks, are carefully hanging on a bedroom clothes butler. A small alarm clock that reads 6:28 a.m. is on a nightstand jammed next to his bed. Some wrinkled sheets reveal an arm exposed to the shoulder leading to the peaceful face of a sleeping Felix Xavier Cole.

The alarm clock rings. F. X. Cole's eyes gently open, and a gentle smile comes over his lips. He sits perched on the edge of his bed. He rises and walks toward the window, pulling the shade cord, allowing an eruption of light to flood the room. He spreads his arms and greets the day to crescendo like an emperor—phoenix rising.

Felix Cole can awaken from deep slumber with absolutely no past residue of sleep appearing on his face at all. This odd manifestation has been going on for the last six months. So vitalized is he upon awakening that he immediately wakes up roused and rushes into a course of action, carrying out the day's agenda. He thought, in the beginning, when he first became aware of this abrupt awakening that this might be a bit peculiar, a play of nerves or some slight anxiety. But he soon wrote it off as a will to self-discipline, a byproduct some simple flotsam dispelled, due to a moral code he has been strenuously developing for himself—a proper exercise for the endurance needed to survive the end of the world.

Felix X. Cole walks briskly over to the bathroom and disrobes. Adjusting the shower water, he looks over at a novelty gadget he has suction-cupped to his shower wall. It is a temperature thermometer that registers the steam heat to assure the water is an accurate degree of 99 to 101. That is slightly warmer than the body temperature of 98.6. The water spews through a special nozzle that simulates a pulse flow in cadence to a pregnant woman's biorhythms. According to the manufacturer's package information, the procedure restores the feeling of being in the womb through pulsating massage. It not only helps you relax; it opens you to experience prewomb embryonic memory that has been dormant during your adult life.

"I have no doubt," Cole mentioned in more than one of his lectures, "that pre-embryonic trauma and pleasure have played more than a passive role in our psychological development, especially in the area of phobias and religious beliefs."

Felix X. Cole steps into the shower station and adjusts the flow valve to a normal pulse. This simulates the pulsing heartbeat to the speed an embryo would experience if a normal mother just exists on an average day with no anxieties.

"On page 15 of the information booklet," Cole ponders aloud to himself, "this setting is best for morning preparation or after a light meal because the digestive tract is most relaxed and not churning away—reducing internal process activity, creating a less likelihood of whipping into a frantic soup over produced acidic bile."

Throwing back his head, he accesses the warm waters of the womb to take him away.

While he is lathering, he notices some hair strands stuck to his soap and a circular cluster around the drain.

"Of course, it is not unusual for a man turning toward midlife to find a few more hairs than usual coming off in the comb or shower floor," he laments, reasoning aloud. "It was one more imperfection to deal with. Not to worry."

Cole accepts it by doing a meditative chant, virtually regressing himself back to the womb. After shaving, he examines his balding head. He removes a partial toupee from its stand and places the synthetic pompadour onto his scalp. Making the necessary adjustments, he checks his look in the mirror.

It might be time for plugs, he thinks to himself. It might be time for plugs indeed.

After committing to the final decision of installing hair plugs, he resumes dressing.

Cynthia Evans is sitting at her kitchen table eating a bowl of granola watching a TV game show. As the program cuts to a commercial, she spins around to her phone to speed-dial her boss, Felix X. Cole. The phone rings three times and goes to the answering machine.

"Good Morning, Dr. Cole, it's me, Cynthia," Cynthia responds. "Just calling to remind you about Sampson Hall today, 1:00 p.m. See you tomorrow. Bye."

Cynthia has been Felix Cole's secretary for three years, and except for when he lectures, she is at her desk, answering phones, setting appointments, and Helping Dr. Cole with the minutiae of his life. They share a good working relationship—Cole is an easygoing boss and Cynthia is more than competent.

A graduate of Brooks Business Academy, Cynthia is an over-thirty, reasonably attractive, active city girl who never had time for a serious relationship. She fell in love just once.

Harry was a hell of a nice person and the piano player at the Wynn–Edwards Country Club—a notorious mob hang out. Harry was the one guy who treated her nicely. They went on romantic cruises and fancy restaurants where he knew everybody; he was familiar with the swankiest places and exclusive dives, mostly because he performed at them.

He would tote her around while "working the room," as he once quipped.

This annoying quirk he had of parading her around bothered Cynthia very much. Harry always seemed to be onstage. Cynthia felt a certain falsity about him, something intuitive she could not explain.

An invisible agenda made her uncomfortable when they were in public. It was getting to the point where a simple walk together arm in arm down a street would make Cynthia feel like an empty arm decoration. She did, however, crave the attention after a while and was able to substitute this hollowness of character in exchange for the romantic charge incurred from the spontaneous visits to cheap motels. In those days, tacky heart-shaped bathtubs and mirrors were endearments of opulence. Cindy thought Harry was Elvis.

Despite all of Harry's meretricious endearments, for the most part, he certainly did fill a void in her otherwise humdrum love life. He would surprise her with jewelry and flowers.

He got in trouble with the mob over some borrowed money issues and left town. Cynthia never heard from him again.

While looking over Dr. Cole's appointment book, Cynthia notices the name Jason Marz highlighted in bright fluorescent green. Mr. Marz, to the best of Cindy's knowledge, is Dr. Cole's oldest—if not the only—friend. He would sometimes drop in unexpectedly—"out of the blue," as they say—bringing coffee and donuts, always pleasant treats for an office girl.

In the event Dr. Cole was not seeing a patient, they would chat in his office or go to lunch. F. X. Cole, not being a very social man, mostly limited it to office chat. Cindy could see that Jay's visits always brought a genuine smile of contentment to Dr. Cole's otherwise trite, weary business face, as *genuine* was not a trait forthcoming to Felix X. Cole.

"Jay," as he insisted she call him during his last visit, left her with a slight thrill of anticipation of his next arrival. The mild flirtation of asking her to address him by the casual brevity of Jay sent a surge of arousing checks and balances through her switchboard of emotional skill sets. As part of her professional acumen, Cynthia has made it a rule not to mix business with pleasure. She never dates the office clients or pharmaceutical vendors and especially not the patients. Jason Marz, on the other hand, being none of those, was fair game to flirt back with.

A gentle purr escapes her lips. Her hormonal sense is tingling.

Unless you call attention to your presence
who will know you're there?

—Rod McKuen

The Lecture

Hartman University sits on a sprawling acreage of hilly greens and walking paths. One might think of the poet Rod McKuen in a cardigan sweater or Arnold Palmer staring down the green plotting a hole in one. The parking lot is plush with the rewards of academic life. Status cars and private parking spaces inspire students throughout; "if you will it, it can be yours" is the message. The medium is institutional architecture, a cloister of laurel trees and grants issued indiscernible modern sculpture.

Students shuffle along, carrying books. Couples mingle, talking on the lawn between classes. Rows of trees are dividing space, as jutting, shiny angles of contemporary art confuse the senses with heady awareness and abstract ambiguity. Nevertheless, traditional Stoic and severe statues of great thinkers still have a home greeting visitors at the entrance with eerie approval.

A bronze effigy to Gertrude Stein imposes her generous, matronly girth over a desk as she appears to be laboring away on some letters. It blocks the sun, casting a shadow over the broad concrete base of her statuette. A student tagged a graffiti post, declaring "ANDREA M. IS MOST LIKELY TO SUCKSEED"—demonstrating once again that the words of the prophets are not written only on the subway walls and tenement halls but are alive and well in the halls academia as well.

Graffiti originated in ancient Italy as inscriptions and drawings marking thoroughfares and walls. Some forms of the hieroglyphics was discovered in 1851 at the ruins of Pompeii. Painting on sidewalks and other forms of graffiti is still common in Rome today as well as most parts of the media-affected world.

Whereas Romans consider graffiti a form of urban art, graffiti has been a thorn in the side of the university grounds maintenance department for a long time. It seems that new students every year feel the compulsion to mark their territory in different ways, sometimes in choices not recognized as art at all. A considerable amount of a groundkeeper's idle time is now being spent scrubbing and whitewashing unsightly paint.

A brick stairway opens up to huge wooden doors that project success and upward mobility. In a few minutes, Alexis Barrette will be ascending these steps to meet her hero, Felix X. Cole

Meanwhile, on the other side of the campus green, two professors meet in front of a whitewashed billboard that reads,

LECTURE ON THE TRADITIONAL MORES EXTINCTION OF MARRIAGE

FEATURED SPEAKER: DR. FELIX X. COLE

DR. COLE WILL ALSO BE DISCUSSING HIGHLIGHTS FROM HIS NEW BOOK

TODAY AT SAMSON HALL, 1:00 P.M.

Beneath, it someone scrawled,

I SCREWD ANNE! —ACE GINZO

SAMMY WAS HERE

LOWRIDER "NOTHING FOREVER"

Beneath that, someone scrawled,

^^SCREWED/CORRECT SPELLING.

(ENGLISH DEPT. 101)

Profs. Jeffery Devore and Jules Valentine are strolling along the grounds on their way to the registrar's office when they notice the advertisement featuring Professor Cole's lecture at Sampson Hall. They casually take note of it earlier from an advert in the Hartman newsletter but pay it no real seriousness. Unfortunately, Felix Cole had become somewhat of a pariah to his academic alumni since he left the campus life in pursuit of private practice. His reputation for being standoffish has left him high and dry and somewhat persona non grata, as far as anything "university" was concerned.

Jeffery Devore is a professor in anthropology and the head of some departments that drew very little attention to anyone outside Hartman walls. Jules Valentine, on the other hand, is actively engaged in media art studies and journalism. Both fellows are fantastic liberals and take part in any cause that would keep the country on the brink of Marxism, thus bringing them into the fold with as many protesting naked female students as possible. For example, they recently attended a rally for body painting in which young female students were having their breasts and buttocks painted in the name of freedom for accepted natural art forms.

Their thoughts about Cole's Lecture went something like this:

"This is an interesting fellow, this Dr. Cole. Do you know much about him?" Professor Valentine inquires.

"I met him once at a dinner for the National Geographic club some time ago, egotistical bird. I always had the feeling he was snickering at me under his breath. He has a strange idea about liberating the world of traditional values," Jeffery Devoe responds accordingly.

"He should have stayed in academia where he would have been labeled 'eccentric' or 'opinionated' instead of a quack in the private sector," Professor Valentine adds.

Jeffery Devore turns and begins walking away in an exaggerated gait.

"Hey, where are you going?" Valentine asks.

"Lecture hall, of course," Devore answers. "It is almost one o'clock. they usually put out a decent buffet for these kinds of things. Maybe sandwiches will be provided."

"Pickles and slaw are more likely to be left," retorts Valentine. "Students are like vultures over deli food."

Professor Devore lets go of a belly laugh so harrowing, it caused a gathering of lawn birds to take flight.

"And mating like monkeys when old Cole is done with them," Devore adds.

He takes up a comfortable jog and joins his partner as they head off to Sampson Hall to catch the show.

Felix. Cole arrives at the Sampson Hall auditorium at 11:30 a.m. He is always early for his appointments, a trait his mother instilled into him at an early age.

"Felix," she would say in a stern voice, "a stitch in time saves nine."

To this day, he still has not a clue what that saying had to do with anything.

He comes in through the door on the street-side entrance, wheeling his books behind him. The slight stoop in his posture diminishes his actual size by about two inches, making him appear not as tall as he is. During his collegian days, he stood a slim six feet three. Cole never excelled in physical prowess. Nevertheless, he carried himself like a jock. He enjoyed fencing, however, and won some awards for the university swordsmanship team, of which he was Captain.

The only other person present in the large empty room is a custodian setting up chairs. The noise of chairs opening and clanging together fills Cole with a brief sense of nostalgia, incurring dizziness, some youthful reverie, bringing to mind a triumph of past valor.

In a trancelike stupor, he murmurs, "The old ghost that seals memories comes forth now and again, whispering our lines, reminding us of the role we play."

He shakes it off. Cole lets himself into a room off to the side prepared for the guest speakers. He removes his coat and hangs it on the back of a chair. The custodian is now pushing the podium in front of the makeshift stage platform.

The lecture hall was far from what the name implies. Gone were the days when lecture halls were booming auditoriums with solid mahogany lecterns and the musty aroma of old books. Grand, dusty old paintings once hung on the walls. Olympian patriarchs long forgotten were now retired to dust and memory themselves, banished to archive rooms and storage bins.

Cole's thoughts are cut short by the procession of a food cart and caterers. The beggar's banquet has arrived. A noisy caravan of food servers bungles their way across the floor. Three more custodians, tack and tape ready, follow along, pulling a long, lengthy banner to hang. The banner reads, "Stanley the Ham and Egg Man and Soup."

Behind the huge letters is a portrait of a Slavic-looking man wearing a cap with twinkling blue eyes and a pirate smile. He is holding a tray of egg sandwiches and a bowl of steaming soup. A green soupy substance spilled over the side. Although he is smiling, he is also sweating, perspiration being demonstrated by tear-shaped dashes of paint flying from his head. He appears to be trotting, implying that he hurries to please his customers.

Stanley's Food Truck was the first food establishment to sell food on campus and to this day is a historic American Dream story.

Stanley Godowsky came to America after the war—World War II, the big one. Naturally, as the story goes, Stanley came here with two bits in his pocket, he got a job working in a Polish deli where he learned English and how to make a good ham-and-egg sandwich. When he saved enough money, he bought himself a secondhand truck from Tony the iceman. Tony, a jack-of-all-trades, helped him convert it into a quasi–hot dog truck. If Tony would have had an epitaph, it would have been this: "I can do many things well but not any one thing great." Stanley kept that quote over his cash register until his truck was broken into one night by neighborhood thugs. The cash register was destroyed, and Stanley eventually forgot about replacing Tony's quote. And so on.

Stanley set up shop on the corner of Hartman place, home to Hartman High School. After acquiring some local notoriety selling his ham-and-egg sandwiches to the teachers and working folks, eventually, he befriended Moe the Bagel Guy and a few other suppliers of lunchmeat products. It was not long before he became known as Stan the Ham-and-Egg Man. Within a few years, fortune had thrown into his path Sophie Verbouski, a local girl whose parents have emigrated from Czechoslovakia.

Every night after skinning the ham shanks, he would save the bone and bring it to Sophie's apartment on request where she lived with her mother. He noticed that she was using his leftover ham bones to make a terrific pea soup. It was a match made in heaven. After they were married, Stanley changed the name of the business from "Stanley the Ham-and-Egg Man" to "Stan the Ham-and-Egg Man and Soup." It was another success.

Stan the Ham-and-Egg Man and Soup . . . and Sophie became so successful that when Hartmann High School became Hartmann College in the booming 1950s, Stanley was able to prevent his thriving enterprise from being ousted of its original street location from the college board, by giving payola to city hall officials. Later on still, when the college gave birth to Hartmann University, Stanley and Sophie were so rich that with the help of some lawyers and politicians, they were able to donate a park and garden to the university to prevent the university from once again trying to throw them off that corner. They named it Dean Park, after Dean Godowsky, their son.

Stanley and Sophie hoped Dean would take over the business one day. Unfortunately, their only prodigy turned out to be a dullard and lackey who wanted nothing to do with the business. He sold it to Sophie's niece who, by coincidence, was named Sophie also. She ran it as a catering service and planned on changing the name very soon to Sophie's Choice Catering. Dean became a full-time surfer. He inherited the family fortune and resided in Venice Beach, California.

The clock on the wall of Sampson Hall reads 3:00 p.m. It has now been two solid hours into the lecture "The Mores of Tradition and the Extinction of Marriage." An unflinching, unblinking droning Professor Cole reaches for his water bottle, refreshing his throat with a welcome gulp. The water rejuvenates his awareness because he has been proselytizing for the last twenty minutes, completely off script.

Intellectual types of all kinds are sitting scattered in rows, mostly nodding their heads, looking bored. Some are sleeping. Some are taking notes. A photographer takes a picture. A few students are eating sponge cake. It would be safe to say that the sleep-inducing effect of tryptophan in the turkey wraps with cream cheese was enough to put out the audience. However, the safer bet would be that Cole's lecture was a few sandals short of a shindig.

Cole looks up from the podium and closes with his final statement.

"And with that, ladies and gentlemen, the territorial spider monkey—not so unlike us—goes back to its role in a communal society. Thank you all for coming today."

The applause was the sound of uneasy people rumbling in their seats as opposed to one hand clapping.

Cole leaves the podium and walks over to the book-signing table, shamelessly waiting to be met by his peers and fellow psychiatrists. He stands by the table, smiling and fishing for compliments. Faculty and students rush past him to get out the door with complete indifference. A student is eating a sandwich as he rushes past Cole. The custodian is now packing leftovers for dinner.

Alexis Barrette, looking over her shoulder, exits the room, shyly standing in the hallway, waiting for Professor Cole to come out.

Cole finds himself looking around the naked chamber, surrounded by the small arsenal of busy custodians folding the chairs and helping themselves to the leftover buffet. Voices are heard in the echoing room complimenting the potato salad. Professor Cole remembers he has to make a stop at the admin office before leaving. It was imperative that he hand over notes on the lecture and drop off some books for the library.

He exits past the custodians into the hallway. He approaches the elevator. While waiting for the door open, a fresh young student named Alexis Barrette decides to make her move, anxiously approaching him to get her book signed.

Alexis walks up to Professor Cole and asks, "Excuse me, sir, I hope I'm not holding you up, Professor Cole. Can I ask you to sign my book?"

Cole looks at Alexis from over the rim of his glasses, takes the book from her, and studies the title. It reads, "Traditional Marriage and the Instinctual Commune of the Spider Monkey by F. X. Cole."

"An older copy," he mentions. "This was my first book."

Cole begins to scribble something into the book.

Alexis Barrette looks on in blushing admiration, ardently in awe of Felix X. Cole's genius. This is a decisive moment. How can she tell him everything she feels in just a few sentences?

"I love your work and your ideas about mating habits," she spurts out, trying to think of something to say. "I found your lecture very provocative, also to be most inspiring."

Never being one to mince words or waste time with small talk on students, Professor Cole replies hastily, "Yes yes. Thank you so much, I am sorry, but I am late for a meeting. Thanks again for attending."

The elevator door opens, and Dr. Cole steps inside, letting the door close in the young woman's face.

Alexis looks down at the book and opens it to the page where Cole signed it. She is excited and awestruck to read,

Thank you and good luck.

As always,
Dr. F. X. Cole

Under it, there is a quick scribbled drawing of a spider monkey hanging from a tree branch with its tail sticking up, exposing a large anus.

The student's face changes from a look of admiration to a look of perplexity. She looks up from the drawing then to the elevator, not knowing what to make of it.

"He didn't even ask me my name," she says to herself.

She frantically pushes the Open button. The elevator door slides open. Removing a felt marker from her bag, she steps into the elevator and writes on the inside door,

FELIX COLE IS A BALD ASSHOLE

Alexis Barrette can now add poetry to her long list of academic achievements. Next to it, she draws a picture of a monkey with a smiling face. Revenge graffiti continues to be the most gratifying art form there ever was.

A New Chapter

The Lyceum Building is a converted old factory considered by some old-timers to be a landmark of the community. It came into existence through humble roots and serendipity. A young woman by the name of Ethel Spencer and her best friend, Dorothy Keats, were coming of age around 1936. Having just completed their courses the prior year, the two budding debutants—now graduates from Hartmann College—were free from schoolwork for the first time in years. As fate would have it, their newfound freedom brought with it the deflated expectations of having to find jobs.

Everything they were qualified for was out of town. Dorothy was already working part-time at Woolworths. Ethel was more of a dreamer. She would always be listening to music and changing her hairstyle. While the girls were shopping one afternoon for pajamas, serendipity raised its capricious head. Ethel Spencer was enlightened with the idea that it would be fun to design some very provocative lingerie and sell them to burlesque dancers. Since most clothing of that kind sold only in underground shops of the day, Ethel thought it would be exciting to bring it more into the mainstream. Not unusual to most women of that era, both girls had a basic understanding of sewing and materials such as lace, satin, and silk. It was only a small leap of imagination to transform a drab housecoat or cotton gown into an erotic Hollywood fantasy of lace panties and flimsy bra corselettes.

They easily incorporated there resources and the skills they acquired from home economics class to open the very first exotic lingerie shop in town. They called it the Eyeceum: A Peekaboo Shop for Adult Women.

Through the early years, the girls withstood a barrage of angry protests. The shop was boycotted and burned to the ground by angry women's groups twice but was always rebuilt by what Dorothy referred to as "the Friends of Ethel and Dorothy Foundation." This was composed of volunteer carpenters, union workers, and people—mostly men—who just wanted to hang around.

During the war years, the Eyeceum converted its factory to assist the US Military during World War II. The seamstresses and material handlers manufactured two things, parachutes and pigeon bras—or, as they are referred to in polite society, pigeon *vests*, made out of bra-like materials and designed for paratroopers to strap to their chests. These were equipped with courier pigeons trained to relay messages back to the base. After landing in a drop zone, the paratrooper would undo his pigeon's bra, load the bird with a message, and send it back to home base. By helping out on the home front, the gals got so many local folks involved in local productivity that naturally, when the boys came home from war, every young bride wanted to surprise him with a peekaboo nightgown from the Eyeceum.

A marquee sign hung on an easel in front of the store window, touted by a smiling mannequin wearing the Venus in Lace design, which read,

> How ya gonna keep 'um down on the farm after they
> have seen Paris?
> Let Ethyl and Dorothy solve that quandary for you.

The Eyeceum flourished for many decades, splintering off into public ownerships and catalog sales, licensing, and brand name changes, until the gals finally passed on. They died filthy rich, loaded. Ethel caught the big casino in '79. She was never married. Dorothy died in a mysterious boating accident off Boca Raton where she was vacationing with a younger lover.

The original building still stands. A hallmark architectural structure—it stood three floors high made of steel and brick, resistant to most fires, with an air raid shelter in the basement. Changing hands over the years, real estate investors thought it would be a good idea to keep the name but change the spelling. It became the Lyceum Building a few years after their deaths.

A memorial dedicated to the two ladies spans the hallway. Historic photos that found on the premise now hang in the hallway. A black-and-white portrait hangs in the lobby of Ethel and Dorothy receiving a plaque from a forgotten mayor.

City hall, not to be outdone, has its favorite pictorial layout. In the meeting room for the chamber of commerce, there is a portrait of a different mayor—long since forgotten—holding a drink and wearing a Shriner's Fez cap while squeezing Dorothy's ass.

The third floor of the Lyceum Building, since its rebirth, is home to the professional counseling services. Because of the altitude and the calming effects of long windows and cityscape vistas, it is ideal for the contemplative arts. All the serious psychologists, advisors, and counselors from around town aspire to one day occupy office space on the third floor of the Lyceum Building at some point in their careers. The plush carpeting and carefully selected artwork send a gentle and subliminal message to all who come for a visit. The advert graffiti, if there were one for this floor, would read something like, "Leave your psyche with us, and we will mindf&*$ you." Most people cannot wait to get into the act.

While the third floor has its more cerebral qualities, the first floor of the Lyceum Building incorporates financial servers and brokers. There are nicknames for the first floor like "steam closet" and "pressure cooker." It is no secret that the boys from floor 1 want to dominate the whole building—moreover, the world. These are the minor masters of the universe. If John Milton waxed poetic for his most defiant angel, "It is better to rule in hell than to serve in Heaven," then the epitaph for boys on the first floor would be, "If I am to be a large fish in a small pond, then fuck it! I'll drink the pond."

The most striking feature in their corporate design is that everything they want you to see is big, unbridled opulence. Besides, everything they are going to do to you is small, like fine print. The graffiti message here is simply laid out, "The large expensive artwork on the walls giveth, the wallpaper taketh away."

However, due to the water main pipe plumbing problem going on in the basement, the third floor is temporarily sharing its empty office space with the first floor. Some writers or poets might compare this uncomfortable dilemma to a modern-day fall from grace. But the folks on the third floor just think of it as bad luck. Both parties involved don't have much time for lofty artistic analysis.

The first floor of the Lyceum Building is alive with the morning flow of busy people crisscrossing in unison with all the orderly gridwork of, again, a Mondrian painting. These are working ants rushing past each other, meeting for appointments and deadlines. They skillfully juggle coffee and contracts while aggressively climbing steps and stampeding in and out of offices to rhythms of pumped-in Muzak. A first-floor information desk clerk once penned the quote

> They all suffer from the three S's—stress, stamina, and sunlight deprivation, the *D* in the acronym eliminated, for time restraint reasons.

This handmade sign still hangs behind his desk until this day.

A woman possessing a well-shaped behind, clad in a snug, fitting, and professionally tailored cotton grey skirt, steps out of the mailroom, undulating her way to the office down the hall. She is hurrying to avoid the eye contact of her temporary new neighbors from the first floor. Bobbing and weaving through the mosaic embroidery wheel of tartan plaids and pinstripes, she races ahead of a newbie office boy nearly knocking a stack of papers from his hands.

Swinging a folder, she immediately veers off, making her way through an office door. The sign on the door reads,

JASON MARZ, GROUP THERAPIST, COUPLES' COUNSELING SERVICES

Once inside, Karen Mitchell holds the folder to her chest and exhales a deep breath, composes herself, and walks toward her boss Jason Marz's office.

Karen Mitchell was not one to eavesdrop on a patient's visit. She was a professional and an all-around good gal. She follows celebrity gossip and is a wiz at crossword puzzles. For the most part, when not occupied with office duties, she reads local magazines and checks her email. Nevertheless, this one instance, when she approached Jason Marz's office, she hesitated and paused to listen before knocking to go in. Putting her ear closer to the door, this is what receptionist Mitchell heard. (Unlike a receptionist, we can go through walls and doors. Let's play the fly on the wall, shall we?)

Jason Marz has an office that is not unlike his personality. In his personal life, he exudes a keen sense of genuine hospitality that comes through in his professional life as well. Somber beiges and browns warm the room. Framed graduate certificates and standard credentials are clearly in view. A bookcase stocked with journals and literature establish trust and confidence, assuring his clients that they can feel safe discussing the facts of their life with a stranger. Although the coffee machine is in the waiting room, a water cooler and a full box of tissues are just an arm stretch away to accommodate distraught clients in their moment of need.

Jason is sitting at his modest desk, hands folded, across a couple, man and woman. A conversation is already in progress.

They are sitting quietly, looking at each other in awkward silence, taking a breather, gathering their senses. Their faces are silly and uncomfortable. The man is Mr. Lenny Watts. Mr. Watts is forty-six years of age. He is wearing a neck and back brace, with a metal walker beside him. The woman beside him, at a comfortable distance, is Laura Watts his wife. Mrs. Watts is a woman of forty-two, a well-dressed woman who keeps herself in good shape. She is looking ahead at Jay, straining not to look at her husband. She is holding a small pile of papers on her lap.

"Mr. Marz, this isn't easy for me," the man broke the silence. "In the beginning, we did everything together. We went everywhere. The money is good, but the job has many occupational hazards attached to it. I cannot help it. I always had high-risk jobs."

"Not 'occupational hazards,' Lenny, you are hazard prone," Laura breaks in. "You are clumsy, overweight, and you are losing body parts constantly. After that thing two years ago with the finger . . ."

Laura reaches over and grabs Len's wrist, holding up his hand to Jason. The ring finger of Len's hand is a prosthetic replacement made of wood with a wedding ring fitted on to it.

Trying to turn his head unsuccessfully, Lenny pulls his hand away from his wife.

"That was not my fault. It was due to a ministroke, damn it!" Lenny retorts. "We have the medical receipts. You have been to the doctor with me."

"I don't care," Laura says, composing herself. "We never had any children because of accident number 3, remember that one? I have it right here."

She rumbles through her paperwork and pulls from the pile a typed sheet of documentation. She scans over the list.

"Aha! Here it is. 'Cause of incident—low-dose radiation exposure.' Because your safety suit was not put on properly. There it is, Mr. Marz., notarized and sealed by OSHA. Yep, all there in black and white. See right here, the little addendum? 'Due to clothing malfunction.' Open zipper. 'Neglect in wearing properly—'"

"Now wait a minute, Laura!"

With tension and voices beginning to rise, Jason is forced to stand up and intervene.

"Please let's take a moment," Dr. Marz tries.

Laura shouts, throwing her hands into the air.

"Take a moment."

"Stick it up your ass!"

Jason's head rears back. His eyelids flicker as he bites his top lip. There is a moment of silence as Laura, shaking her head in desperation, begins nervously assembling her paperwork.

"This is a mistake by coming here," Laura voices. "I have about thirty good years of my life left, and I am not going to spend them taking care of you. I do not need a marriage counselor I need a lawyer. I am out of here."

Lenny twists and pivots to try and bring Laura back but is unable to reach her. During the mayhem, Lenny's therapeutic roller is pushed out of reach due to the inertia of gravity and his body weight. He lunges for it, losing his balance, and falls to the floor.

Crawling around, Lenny snags his sleeve on the chair coaster, toppling it to the floor almost on top of him. Laura is sidestepping the whole mess with the agility and grace of a stage performer and whips the door open to find receptionist Karen Mitchell crouched over with her ear on an air cloud where the door used to be.

Ms. Mitchell gasps in surprise as Laura Watts huffs past her. Jay comes around from his desk and struggles to pick the large man up from the floor. He brushes him off and seats him.

After a few moments of composure, Jay and the man exchange uncomfortable glances.

Karen looks on, clutching her folder, biting her lip.

Lenny, huffing and puffing, looks up at Jay from the chair.

"I guess I am going to need a lawyer," he huffs.

Jay poises himself on the edge of his desk, looking on sympathetically.

Without much more to say, Lenny asks, "Am I going to be billed for this visit?"

The sun was setting earlier. The fall sky brought with it a delicate hue of periwinkle mauve that lent the effect of impressionism to the air. Muted grays and silver sidewalks bordered asphalt streets. Pinpricks of light salted the skyline as tenement buildings slowly begin coming to life—first, one by one, then a few at a time.

Jason sips his coffee, watching the street unfold from the café window of the Clarion supermarket. He looks at his watch, and it reads 4:45 p.m. He is walking, around daydreaming for an hour and a half.

Where does the time go? he muses to himself.

Moving his cart to the check-out line, Jay takes a spot in the cue and waits.

The somnambulist cashier punches numbers into a machine as customers swipe plastic cards or pay with cash. As Jay waits, he could not help noticing the posse of shoppers slowly circling him. The lines fill up with rush-hour customers. He begins to feel mildly suffocated from the presence of overbearing people. His eyes jitter from cart to cart and person to person. Unexpectedly his pulse speeds up, and he could feel a thumping rhythm at his temples; waves of heat flashes spread across his shoulders then down his spine. His lungs feels like an accordion, with holes punched through it. He imagines for a moment that his breathing might sound like bizarre wheezing so he attempts to loosen his tie, focusing on a shopping cart to distract his mind from the obvious anxiety attack he was experiencing.

There are cascading boxes of cereal and potato chips, canned soups, and rolls of toilet paper that seem to be multiplying and overflowing. He becomes critically aware of the shape and size of each item with an acute paranoia that seizes his entire being. Every second begins to feel like an eternity.

A bunch of celery tightly compressed by a rubber band protrudes from a plastic bag. Jay begins counting each stalk that make up the bunch, just to keep from passing out. He gets to four and has to turn away as a brief surge of nausea wells up inside him. After what must have been only a few seconds of extreme psychic chaos, he hears the cashier call him.

"Will, that be all, sir? Did you find everything you were looking for?'

"Yeah, thanks," he barely answers back, struggling to catch his breath.

Resuming some normal judgment, Jay is able to conjure up enough attention to complete his transaction. Becoming increasingly self-conscious of his awkwardness, Jay gathers up his bag and follows the cue to the exit. Once outside, he rests for a moment to gather his thoughts.

The chilly air feels good inside him as he focuses on his breathing. His face begins to cool, and soon Jason Marz was normal—even feeling aware that he would now have to button his coat.

It's good to feel cold, he muses.

The streets begin to fill with the rush-hour crowd. The anxious working class jettisons from sidewalk to sidewalk, hurrying to their destinations. A flock of migrating birds adds an aerial act to the scene as they cross the autumn sky en route to their winter havens.

Jay walks up a brick staircase to his apartment door, sets down his groceries, fumbles a key into the lock, and pushes open the door to his brownstone apartment. Now securely inside, he leans on the kitchen table and draws a breath. It was not often that he has panic attacks, not since during the last few years since Donna.

Anyway, he was home. Jay feels good to have a familiar dwelling place to come to. It is quiet. The phone hardly ever rings. That is a hard thing to get used to, not hearing the phone ring with a predictable check-in call.

To think that at one point, he began to get annoyed at the humdrum convention of the call, how it would always strike at the most inopportune moment. "Hi, how was your day? Is everything okay?" alternatively responding to the most mundane concern for his well-being with curt, snippy replies and abrupt dismissal. Absence has a way of making you yearn for second chances.

Jay's apartment is a comfortable converted brownstone that he was able to get through a friend who was moving out of town and offered him the opportunity to take over the lease. Jay has always loved brownstones, and at the time when Donna was around, it was going to be their nesting place. The irony still haunts him now; and then of the perfect timing—the engagement, the opening of his practice, and Donna's rising achievement as a chef—all seemed to follow a fairy-tale sequence that unfortunately lacked the fairy-tale ending.

The apartment is neat and orderly. A pleasant balance of eclectic contemporary furniture and comfortable art makes up his cozy dwelling. The jewel in the crown, however, is the kitchen.

Before Jay met Donna, just out of night school, like most single men, Jay had never given much thought to a kitchen, except for it being a place to open a box of cereal or to heat some Chinese noodles. A kitchen was a little more than a refueling station to grab a quick bite on your way out the door to a part-time job or a friend's performing-arts gig somewhere. A kitchen, for the most part, was a place that Jay thought only his mother would have an interest. It was not until Donna came into his life that his myopic view of adulthood opened up.

One instance Jay frequently recalls is of having to accompany Donna to a special event her parents hosted one evening.

They had been dating for only a short time. Donna was so proud to have him agree to go. She wanted so badly to show off her new boyfriend with whom she was crazy about to all her cousins and relatives. However, on his deliverance, he looked like a beatnik college student. She insisted that he make some changes to his hideous wardrobe or the whole night would be a disaster.

There was not a lot of time. Without missing a beat, she grabbed his hand, and they ran to a local thrift store that was across town. Donna took him through the men's clothes department and picked out a clean white shirt, a tie, and a pair of quick-fit slacks. Jay just quickly tried things on, taking direction and feeling like a wardrobe dummy. Donna was able to borrow a jacket from her best friend's brother Danny in half an hour. Jay looked great, and the evening was a success. It was from that one instance out of the many that Jay realized how much Donna completed him.

Everything with Donna was spontaneously brilliant like that. It was due in part to the personality she possessed. She was able to turn a meatloaf into a banquet on a dime. It was the art spirit she possessed in cooking that kept winning her culinary awards throughout her short career. There are cooks, there are chefs, and there are artists. Donna was an artist.

She could smell when delicate sauces were finished; the intensity of a searing pain would inform her when the last ingredient is added. She could judge gourmet meals by color, texture, and aroma the way a skilled draftsman would use line, shape, and form. Her knowledge of French cuisine was vast and sweeping. Her Italian dinners were all-day romantic adventures.

A few seasons have come and gone since those days and nights Jay spent with Donna. When she died an innocent victim of a drive-by shooting, everyone was stunned and moved deeply.

The way it happened was like this: Donna was coming out of a convenience store one evening. It was a neighborhood shop not far from her place of work down the block from the main intersection. She rarely ventured off the main street because of the deteriorating neighborhood, it was not safe to wander around when the sun went down. Being a local girl her whole life, however, Donna still felt as though she knew this town like the back of her hand and perceived no real problem with a quick in-out to a store she had been familiar with her whole life. Swimmers and seafolk adhere to the adage "The better a person can swim, the more likely they are to drown when the undertow gets unpredictable." In short, nature has a way of making an expert look like a fool, if they let their guard down.

One particular evening, nature had it that a gaggle of derelict youth gathered outside, talking with some aging teenagers in a car not far from the Delcy's Convenience Store. Nothing was that unusual or threatening; it was trendy to be fashionably suspicious looking in those days. "Thug life" fashion was so prevalent that it was mandatory for police and local law enforcement not to profile anyone on the way they dressed or presented their actions. As a result, most aging teenagers looked the same—the good, the bad, and the ugly; the old and the young. It was eternal springtime for the criminal element and winter for local law enforcement.

The silence of the evening ended when a large utility vehicle came roaring down the street, spraying storefront windows with Uzi fire. The more seasoned players ducked and fled. A stray bullet, however, landed in Donna's rib cage, severing a lung and a major artery. She died on the operating table.

For a short time, anyone close to Jay and Donna stayed in touch to commiserate; but after a while, as time heals, slowly one by one, those who had no real connection outside the relationship with Jay other than their ties with Donna began taking their rightful place back with the living and resumed with their lives. Jay eventually lost contact with everyone from that circle.

It even became a strain to send an occasional greeting card or hello to Donna's parents. Moreover, it happened when he did not receive a card from Donna's folks who have since moved to Florida. Jay, in turn, lost interest in sending them a card; and so it died. No one ever called or visited. Most of Donna's friends have gotten married, pursuing their own lives. People just became uncomfortable talking about the horror to which others have acclimated. Besides, Jay has nothing new to add.

Jay found himself chording in the company of his one longstanding friend from college, Felix Cole. Cole remained the last friend he could talk with who knew Donna. Jay understood deep down that it was only out of Cole's shortcomings and social faux pas that he lent an ear. Jay always knew Cole to be a reprehensible, soul-depraved human being. However, Jay remained loyal and overlooked it. That was his nature.

When Donna met Felix Cole for the first time, she told Jay.

"His hand was clammy like a trout," she'd often say.

On another occasion, when Jay suggested that he was considering Felix Cole as his best man for their wedding, Donna replied, "That's up to you, Jay, but please keep him on your side of the aisle. He gives me the creeps."

Sometimes the nights would pass like one short recurring dream; others would go on, never ending.

It is a blustery day; all local weather reports seem to predict a winter mix of icy rain and sleet for the evening. With nowhere to go, Jay ponders the wine rack in his kitchen, scanning the modest selection of assorted California reds and Italian chiantis until his finger hits the bottle just to his liking.

Popping the cork with exaggerated ease, he turns his focus to a few favorite CDs he gathered in a basket and pulled a disc from its nest. Within a few seconds, the apartment is magical again, permeated with the soft aroma of wine and soothing light jazz riffs. On the small wall shelf, some handwritten recipe books and photo albums are stacked willy-nilly.

He removes a photo album that contains recipes and pictures, a draft compilation for a cookbook that was never completed. Some cover ideas and food art are pinned together with paperclips, along with ideas and witticisms carefully highlighted across the page. A photo is glued to a blank page. It is a proof copy of a wholesome-looking girl with a chef's outfit and hat, a few graduation pictures from Laird's Culinary Institute, and photos of Jay and this girl kissing. Other photos show off food dishes and clowning around in the kitchen—dozens of photos explaining the rich life he had shared with his one true love.

The ingredients that go into a relationship are a fine balance of sincerity, soul bearing, and respect. The proportions of cannot always be duplicated from person to person—if someone leaves the cake out in the rain, as the song goes. There is no guarantee you can ever get that recipe right again.

Speaking to himself aloud, Jay utters, "Ah! Donna's orange chicken with sage and fall veggies. That will work."

After the tragedy, cooking became a home therapy for Jay, helping to ward off the ennui of lonely nights. The gentle effort of gathering ingredients, along with the cohesion of sweet memories, was a soothing balm at the end of a long day.

He placed his fingers to his lips and passed a kiss to the photo. Turning in an about-face, he heads back to the main kitchen to prepare the meal.

Since Jay was always independent, he became a very good cook. His mother became ill at an early age and was not always able to prepare large meals. Jay's older brother married and moved away to pursue a career, and his father died from complications of a ruptured hernia when Jay was seventeen. This forced him to step into the role of man of the house by proxy. Jay's thoughts of family life pretty much formulated into one of cold, utilitarian responsibility compared to the Rockwell-Ian portrayals of garnished long tables and American family pride.

It wasn't until Jay had met, lived with, and fell in love with Donna that he got his first inkling about how love made a home. Through Donna, Jay was able to explore the whole spectrum of emotions that lovers experience in the beginning. She was a promising career girl full of life and whimsy, a prodigy of the American Dream.

Nights like these, he could feel her capricious spirit all around him, transforming their tiny apartment into a Tuscan Villa or a rolling cobblestone alley tavern. Life and contentment could rise from a sauté pan, intoxicating him with the perfume of sage and citrus. Nights like these fill him with every thankfulness a man could bestow on his Creator and curse him in vain at the same time. Because when Donna died, Jay knew he would never replace her. Not only because he strongly believed it was not possible but also because bitterness had won the day. Fate presented itself as an Indian giver, delivering him a gift he could not keep.

Jay walks over to the east window to look out the traffic noise rises from the street below, humming and buzzing in sync with a gentle jazz vibration that fills the room. It is a wondrous revelation when the soul is open to it, how art in its abstract form follows the rhythms of day-to-day events.

Taxi horns stab holes in the quiet pauses between songs.

The onion and garlic are floating nicely over a sheer film of oil as Jay chops the broccoli. Preparing the chicken with orange and sage, Jay artistically begins dressing the bird with the finesse of a cultured apprentice. When everything is roasting and the timer goes off, the humble meal is plated and consumed. Jay tastes the last gulp of wine with the confidence of a man who has learned to enjoy life's pleasures alone.

Rising from the banquet table, he proceeds to the mantle. A business card for Felix X. Cole falls to the floor. He turns it over and finds where he keeps Felix's home number. He makes the call.

Felix X. Cole sits in his armchair watching television. He is wearing a T-shirt and sweatpants and white socks. The growth of his unshaven face is patchy giving him a look of irritability that was avant-garde. Felix is now a master at concealing secrets. He recently adds another one to his bag of tricks. He has been secretly practicing suicide techniques.

Felix has been toying with the idea of ending it all for quite some time now; despite the years of practice in psychiatry, proclaiming this wrong, he just cannot escape the urge to do something harmful to himself.

He thinks of it more as a style of Russian roulette than real suicide, challenging and invigorating. You see, these are not full-blown attempts at taking one's life. If Felix wanted to, he could do it securely and immediately—that is, if he wanted to. Nevertheless, that is not a challenge at all to sly Felix. He hopes to be caught or almost caught doing it. Better yet, he yearns to have it happen as an accident before he or anyone else can prevent it.

Like Russian roulette, at the decisive moment, can you pull the trigger? Besides, if you do, is the empty barrel going to click or will you ride the mind wave of oblivion to the great Kahuna?

Felix Cole is a living game of chance. He is the croupier and the pigeon waiting to clip both in the same person. Every move he makes is another chance. Moreover, he can dangle life and death right under your very nose, and you most likely will not even suspect what he is playing.

If Abraham Cole were not a complete sociopath, then Felix at least shared a gene or two. Felix's father was a cold, calculating man. He had very little sympathy for others and lacked any real sense of emotional love for his wife Elisabeth and his only son young Felix. He was an astonishingly intelligent man for his time and was able to use information in business ruthlessly.

While raising young Felix—a chore he avoided at every turn—he would coldly scold him for anything he deemed to be wasting time. Time and opportunity finally arrived for Felix to be sent abroad, in pursuit of an Ivy League education. Abe Cole did not hesitate in the least to ship him off.

Two years at Chambers Prep Academy offered young Felix three squares and a cot in a military environment with all the study a teenage boy could detest. Upon his return, he resumed studies at a choice college institutional facility where he would eventually meet Jason Marz.

Felix never had any real use for any of it. He can barely remember full sequences of any events from those days. The only vivid memory that still shines in him were the parting words from his father when they dropped him off at the academy: "Your welfare is our concern. Don't fuck this up, Felix. I worked hard for it."

When Abraham Cole died about nine years later, Felix was twenty-two years old. He was out of town on a bender with some aging teenagers he met in New Mexico and was unable to attend the funeral. He was in a bordello shaving a prostitute's wooly alpaca when he got the news.

His mother Elisabeth tried to love her son, but Abraham made it a nightmare. From the beginning, it was doomed. When she told her husband she was pregnant, he blamed her for infidelity, which of course was absurd. Abraham was the only man Elisabeth had ever known in the carnal sense. She was a virgin when they met at Sisters of the Mount Annual Carnival. She was seventeen, and Abraham was twenty-five and already somewhat worldly.

Abe was enjoying a shore leave from the merchant marines and was seeking a bride. Elisabeth fit the bill. She was young, dumb, and somewhat homely. She fell for Abe immediately. His air of confidence and seamen's swagger swept her off her feet, her young mind overflowing with fantasies of high-sea adventure and romance. Being a lusty, self-centered narcissist, Abe just wanted to be adored. They were married.

The marriage from the start was never happy. Elisabeth's parents disliked Abe and accused him of robbing the cradle. Soon after their honeymoon, Elisabeth discovered she had contracted the clap, a surprise Abe brought back from a romp he had with a waitress in the Philippines. It was at that point Elisabeth became completely disgusted with sex.

Whenever Abraham would approach her, she would recoil into a fetal position and cry. Abe began drinking heavily. At times he would fly into a rage, cursing and ranting saying things like "I should have stayed in the Philippines," and then he would go to sleep.

Most of Elisabeth's life with young Felix was trying to keep him out of his father's way. She eventually died of old age. She was sixty. The medical examiner and the funeral director both agreed she had the vagina of a twenty-year-old woman, practically unused. The only endearing thing Felix remembers from his mother was her saying, "If ever there was an Immaculate Conception, son, you are it."

Felix is watching a soap opera. The phone starts ringing. As usual, Felix lets it go to the answering machine. To his surprise, it is his secretary.

"Hi, Dr. Cole, it's Cindy. I just wanted to tell you Jay Marz will be stopping in to see you."

Felix's eyes follow the sound of her voice as his head points up, gyrating like a poodle sniffing invisible roses in the backyard. He waits until she hangs up and continues eating his ice cream.

It is a sunny afternoon, and Jason expects to take full advantage of it. He just has gotten his haircut, his shoes shined, and a new tie. It is a perfect day to visit Mr. Cole and see if he could coax him into an evening get-together for a few drinks.

Jay knows that Cole is occupying a new office on the swanky West Side. Jay has already heard about the new building from where Felix X. Cole was working. It has received a grand review from *Upward Professional* magazine as the new trendsetter location for anybody who is anybody. With that being said, it comes as no surprise to Jay that Dr. Cole who, whenever possible, made it a point to assure everyone that he was of course "the somebody" who would soon be moving into it.

The vestibule has the smell of new flooring and freshly painted walls, unlike the entrance of the Lyceum Building that sometimes reeks of the ectoplasm from the ghosts of Ethel and Dorothy. There is no directory board on the wall as of yet, but there is an information desk to fill the void. Checking his watch, Jay walks over and asks the security guard where he might find the office of Felix X. Cole.

The kindly older gentleman in uniform checks his directory sheet, looking over his bifocals, and answers him, "The fifth floor, sir, you can take the elevator or use the stairs."

He promptly signals in the direction of both.

Still reaping the benefits of a brisk, stimulating day, Jay decides to take the steps and walks up to Felix Cole's office.

While touring the stairwell, Jay steps aside, making way for three young women to pass. As they brush by him, he could smell the mingled scent of perfume and the youthful presence of their demeanor. He also becomes painfully aware that, as polite and courteous as they were, they excuse themselves with the niceties and respect one would show to an uncle or elder of the tribe. In other words, while climbing those stairs, Jay becomes painfully aware he was climbing another kind of hill also—the one where a man approaching middle age realizes young women do not flirt with him anymore. Jay feels he was becoming invisible.

A custodian is sweeping the next landing. He walks up to another flight. Now getting slightly out of breath, a young girl talking on a cell phone races past him. Finally getting to the fifth-floor landing, Jay takes a breath and reaches for the stairway door handle. From behind the door, a bicycle messenger on foot carrying a compact lightweight bike comes blustering through. Excusing himself, he hurries down the steps. Jay thinks to himself that he has become a holding card member of a different generation, one who is continuously obstructing young people on their way to that mysterious place young people go.

Jay stands outside of the stairway exit and looks down the empty hallway. Resting a moment, catching his breath, he proceeds toward Cole's office.

The plaque on the door reads,

DR. FELIX X. COLE, PSYCHIATRIC MEDICINE

Jay grabs the brass handle and goes in. The desk of Cynthia Evans is caddy cornered by a large window overlooking the city. Some waiting chairs are scattered around tables covered with neatly stacked magazines. Gentle ambiance music is lulling in the background.

One gets the feeling, Jay thinks, *of visiting a funeral director.*

As Jay approaches, Cindy looks up and recognizes him instantly. Her eyes widen with surprise as she fidgets to look nonchalant. Cindy has known Jay would be visiting, and no formal arrangement was made.

Defaulting to her woman's intuition, she takes special pains over the last two weeks to make sure her five-point safety checks are all in place—hair, makeup, semisexy slacks, V-neck sweater (revealing just a hint of cleavage), and eau de cologne.

"Well, hello, Mr. Marz. Is Dr. Cole expecting you?" she asks in her most "come hither" tone.

"Hello, Cindy. No, he does not know I am here. But I know he takes his lunch around this time," Jay responds. "I was in the neighborhood, and heck, here I am. Is he in there? Is it a bad time? I can come back."

"He should be in his office having his lunch," Cindy answers, not sure how to respond. "Go ahead in. I'll buzz him and let him know you are here."

Cindy hits the intercom.

"Dr. Cole, Jason Marz is here. Would you like me to send him in?"

Jason begins walking to the door before final affirmation, a liberty most friends feel indulgent in taking.

"Thanks, Cindy," Jay quips.

Proceeding forward, he knocks twice and turns the doorknob to find it locked. There is a rumble of mild commotion, chairs sliding and doors opening and closing. Quick footsteps thump from behind the door. A rattling of locks and awkwardly the door flings open as Jay confronts a disheveled Felix Cole, face to face, in the doorway—his face flushed and his thinning hair tufted on one side. The collar of his shirt is unbuttoned and his tie askew, giving him the appearance of someone just awakened from a nap. If Jay had looked a little closer, he would have noticed a red burn mark on the side of his neck.

Felix is crowding the doorway, slightly nervous, with an uneasy smile. Jay has to push past him to get into the office, and Felix is almost on top of him. Once inside, Jay looks around at his friend's new office in silent admiration.

"Jay, it's good to see you. Sit and make yourself at home," Cole tells him.

While holding the door open, Cole calls out to Cindy to prepare some coffee.

"Jay, let me take your things," Cole says, taking Jason's coat and hanging it on a hook.

As he proceeds toward his desk, the coat falls to the floor, but Cole does not notice it. Jay is jaded to his friend's idiosyncrasies. After the fiasco of trying to get through the door, not wanting to bring any more tension into the room, Jay just let the coat lie there. They both silently ignore it.

Cole excuses himself and briefly leaves the room to help Cindy with the coffee. As Jay is looking around, he notices the utility room door slightly ajar with a swivel chair knocked over. Firmly printed on the seat were two dusty footprints of Cole's thirteen-inch patent leather oxford shoes.

Felix returns with the coffee. Noticing Jay's curiosity, he starts to explain.

"I was adjusting a loose alarm spigot just before you came in," Felix addresses Jay's observation through a nervous giggle. "See it up there. Silly thing hisses now and then. I have to have maintenance look at it."

There was a sturdy long pipe stretched across the closet with a fire safety spigot attached in the middle. The pipe was a strong gauge metal and high enough to suspend a person of Felix Cole's height and weight, if he were ever trying to hang himself with his tie.

"Here sit, sit." Cole places the coffee before Jay and sits down.

"You were standing on that?" Jay responds, pointing to the chair. "You could have fallen and broken your neck."

"Highly unlikely, but yes, I suppose you are right," Cole answers. *Jay Jay, Jay Jay Jay!* It is not often that we get to lunch anymore. Where does all the time go?"

Jay pulls around, scratching his chin. "I wish this were more of a pleasure visit. Some things are bugging me. Can I confide in you, Felix?"

"Sure, fire away, pal. I'm all ears," Cole offers his best attempt at comforting. "You see, you are sitting upright. What do you think of that chair? That is top-of-the-line ergonomics, my boy. I have done away with that whole couch thing—too old fashioned, cliché. I shaved my beard. Have you noticed it? Less Freudian. Fuck all that 'father figure' shit. My clients today hate their fathers anyway. How is your old man, Jay?"

"Dead," Jay answers. "Many years ago."

"Ahh, I'm so sorry to hear that, Jay. Please accept my late condolences," Cole sympathizes. "We are getting older, Jay, and they are getting younger. Nobody wants a stodgy shrink. I am working on some hair plugs too. Do you remember that raccoon thing I was considering? In retrospect—hideous. This is the future in hair-replacement therapy right here, transplants the whole follicle."

Cole gets up and bends forward, bringing his balding pate directly in front of Jay's face.

"See how it's filled in a little more back here?"

Felix leans in and displays the top of his balding head to Jay, circling the implants with his finger.

"See how cleverly they are inserted. They come from the back of my neck, you know."

"Ah, yes, I did notice something different," Jay replies, becoming uncomfortable.

Cindy enters with napkins and places them down, smiling at Jay. She excuses herself and exits the office. Felix hands some napkins to Jay and takes his own. He walks over to the window and looks out.

"I love this new office, Jay. Just look at this view, large windows with a ledge. I always wanted a view like this—pigeons on a ledge, much better than a birdcage. Inch-thick shatterproof glass. It's sealed shut."

"Very impressive, Felix," Jay responds.

Felix pauses, changing his tone to a low, dull, contemplative, monotone voice—his left eyebrow rises in seriousness.

"What is it you wanted to talk about, Jay?"

Jay gets up and starts pacing around the room, pounding his hand into his fist.

"I am beginning to hate my work."

"Come on, Jay. You always had a great enthusiasm for counseling. You are a natural people person. I always thought marriage counseling was ideal for you. You know what they say, those who can't do, teach."

"Thank you, Felix, charming bedside manner. I hope you are gentler with the criminally insane," Jay went on. "I just don't think I can help anybody. I do not believe they want help. Some just want out. Most problems are the result of bad choices. Once made, the couples are stuck with them. Contracts, rules, lawyers—people are not born knowing how to do the right thing. There is a lot of trial and error in a marriage. It would be easier for the more impulsive types, if they could just start over again. Maybe try a few times until they get it right. You know before shit hits the fan and they get so fucking crazy they want to kill each other."

"You mean try marriage a few times 'til you get it right?" Felix interjects. "With my car rental, I get a free oil change. Sometimes they throw in a tire rotation. But, Jay, I don't see what bargaining chips are available."

"I think I am burning out, Felix. After Donna, I do not know. Not one couple comes into my office with the kind of love and respect for each other that Donna and I had. I often wonder if we would have changed toward each other, had we more time. Maybe I am not the one for this. I think of Donna too much. I blame 'professional malaise' routine. Who knows? You ever question what you do, Felix? Do you question the decisions you make? I am not doing anything for anyone that old-fashioned honesty and commitment could not solve. We can theorize over the motivations of selfishness, but the root is still self-centered, not what the clerics call love. The choices people make at one point in their life might not have the same relevance when they outgrow a feeling. Do you ever question your choices, Felix? Would you travel the same road if—"

Jay stops himself midsentence. Briefly looking over, he notices Felix has a deadpan on his face. He seems to be looking out the window, but he is not there. He is squeezing his coffee mug so tightly, it almost breaks in his hand.

Felix is looking out the window, down four floors to the sidewalk. People are gathering, looking at something, huddling around an accident of some kind. At that height, the pedestrians look like small toys. Traffic seems to slow down, as drivers are rubbernecking at the spectacle. However, that is not Cole's point of interest.

On the adjacent corner are four singers performing a quartet singing act. Intensely Cole focuses. He could see them as though they were only a few yards away. It was as if Felix X. Cole was on the other side of the window hovering above the street, watching them. Although the tempered glass windows reduce outside sound, Cole could hear them singing softly, muffled as if they were in the other room. This in reality would have been impossible.

Three of the young male performers are wearing red satin jackets, white shirts, and black pants; while the lead singer was wearing a tan windbreaker, a T-shirt, and jeans. The song is "Red Sails in the Sunset," a song that bears no particular relevance to Cole that he could think of. He thinks he might have heard it a very long time ago when he was a baby. He recalls hearing his mother singing it or maybe he is just imagining it. Nevertheless, at that moment, it is the most beautiful song he has ever heard in his life.

As the crowd began to thin out, Cole notices the black patent leather shoes of a man lying in the street. Cole hovers closer for a better look. It is indeed a well-dressed man just lying in the street with a pencil-thin mustache, smiling. His eyes are wide open; this exaggerates his thick eyelashes, adding to his countenance a campy, feminine stare. His round, chubby face—almost comical—makes him look unusual, like a circus cartoon character rather than a real person. His black suit perfectly fits and tailored; however, on closer inspection, Cole could notice it is made of polyester, with obvious nylon stitching creating a meretricious, cheap, and nauseating effect. He is not dead and does not seem to be hurt, as his hands are folded across his chest, holding red carnations. A nametag on his lapel reads, "Billy."

Felix becomes critically aware that Jay is still in the room. Besides, he feels he should answer him. He says nothing of what he is witnessing.

"You feel the marriage counseling thing isn't for you?" Cole says unexpectedly.

"Felix, are you all right?" Jay asks, knowing his friend. "You look weird."

Reacting like someone who just came out of anesthesia, Felix says, "No, I'm just thinking about something you said—our choices, Jay. You're talking about that demon, rum."

At this point, Cole is struggling with which reality he should put his foot. He is holding on to a swinging Tilt-A-Whirl ride and is, with all his heart, hoping it will stop soon before he screams. Looking at his watch, Felix begins to come to life.

"Ah, Jay, I'm sorry," Cole sputters, becoming very animated. "I hate to cut this short, but I have someone coming in within the hour. Hey, let's get together soon and discuss this maybe over a round of golf."

"Golf? I don't play golf," Jay answers.

"Then how about you and the wife come down to the club. Join me Thursday for dinner, okay?"

Jay is becoming confused.

"Felix, what are you talking about? You know Donna passed away two years ago. I feel like you do not even know who I am. What is going on here?"

Cole becomes more intense.

"Sorry to rush you along, Jay. Nevertheless, this patient coming in is a real hardcase. She experiences intense mood swings. She demands all my attention. At times, I considered calling in an exorcist. I must prepare. Please do call. Maybe we can go to a ball game or something . . . to get your mind off things."

Jay is becoming frustrated.

"A ball game! For crying out loud, Felix. Really?"

Felix escorts Jay out, holding him under the arm, pushing him through the door.

"Cindy, please show Mr. Marz out and get all his information. Jay, I will see you soon, buddy, looking good."

Felix shoots Jay a thumbs-up then closes his office door.

"What information, sir—err…ahh, Jay, Mr. Marz?" Cindy asks Jay, trying to keep up appearances asks.

"It's okay. Jay is fine, Cindy. Don't fret it. He is a little tense about the patient coming in, the difficult case."

Cindy is confused.

"Patient? The next appointment is not until tomorrow morning. That would be Eva, a lovely retired older woman who loves to ramble on about her garden. We call her Eve. She is suffering from Lewy body dementia, a real sweet lady."

Not knowing what to do with the rest of his afternoon, Jay strolls along Broadway, not fully understanding what just transpired between him and Felix. He decides to let it go and just enjoy the gift of this beautiful autumn afternoon. Feeling a little adventurous, he decides to stop into a bar and have a drink to take the edge off.

The green-and-gold sign of the Short Run Inn and the pretty people sitting by the window lure him in. The last of the lunch crowd are leaving, and some stools open up by the window. Jay likes to sit by the window whenever he could so he could people watch. Window seats also provided just the right venue to stare into so you do not have to keep looking around the room appearing lonely, narrowing the opportunity for other lost souls to engage you in conversation.

Although Jay is very friendly and open, he hates it when drunks cry on his shoulder. It has been Jay's experience early on that total strangers not knowing him from Adam would never heed his expert advice while he comforted them at the bar. Nevertheless, if he were charging them for an office visit for the same information, they would think he was a wonderful bolt of knowledge, a compassionate saint overflowing with wisdom. Jay could not help but wonder why people—most people—are more likely to accept bullshit if it has a designer tag attached to it instead of embracing truth from wherever it comes.

The bartender approaches Jay with a friendly hello and takes his order. Thinking of his friend's cryptic reference to rum earlier, Jay orders a rum and Coke. The server is an attractive woman in her midtwenties, with a bright smile and a pleasing glow about her. She has long, flowing, red hair that she kept pulled back to one side with a large hair clip. She is fair skinned like a child making for a perfect painting on canvas or a Degas pastel. On her left shoulder is a cascading tattoo of butterflies and moonbeams traveling down her arm, transforming into a pyramid of smiling skulls just above her wrist.

"Cheers," says the barmaid, gently placing the drink before him.

Jay takes a sip and holds it in his mouth for a second, allowing the smoky caramel mixture of rum and cola to tease his senses.

A friendly bartender can be the source of more than just drinks and a sympathetic ear, Jay surmises. *Sometimes they can be living art.*

The Short Run Inn was a friendly place that still kept the atmosphere of a turn-of-the-century tavern. As hands changed over the years, every new owner put their signature style to the décor in one small way or another. Fortunately, all the owners kept their nuances to a minimum, and no one disturbed the natural beauty and nostalgia of the original landmark design.

The tavern could comfortably seat about a hundred patrons. The handcrafted bar was original rosewood. Mirrors reflected period glassware, and the flooring was original marble and tile. French doors led out to a patio where a band would entertain at night. The indoor dance floor was always freshly polished. In the winter, a fireplace warmed the guests. If it were possible for a building to be a ghost—a living entity that takes on the memories of the ones who have lived and died there—then the Short Run Inn is certainly that because none of the amenities mentioned are in use anymore; they just sell memories.

Most people of the drinking age now stop in to watch a cable sporting event, drink light beer, or bring their laptop to a booth seat, scanning videos that went viral.

Good Night, Rabo Karabekian

Folklore had it that during the Prohibition, rum runners were serving hooch in the wee hours of the night to local gangsters, their girlfriends, and politicians. While mobsters were feasting on their lobsters, local big shots were eating steak and dancing with the girls. From back in the day, the original trap door leading to a secret room still exists behind the Short Run Inn. It added some real history to the place, making good conversation for tourists.

Back in the day, in the event of an FBI raid, the politicians and local bigwigs could hide out until the heat was off. The space was sizable for a converted beer cellar. Some of the amenities it offered the hoodlums were tables, chairs, fans to vent cigar smoke, and a makeshift Frigidaire stocked with cold cuts and condiments. There was a fully stocked bar a couch and a pool table. The room also served as an illicit gambling parlor on Saturday nights. It was a real fun time, until a woman's group against alcohol and whoring tried to burn it to the ground. The stock wood-frame building was soon rebuilt in brick provided by the masons and still stands today.

Later after the war, while the forties and fifties were creating the baby boomers, the Short Run Inn was a first-class restaurant and steak house. It was at that juncture baseball memorabilia and World War II icons hung behind the bar. Autographed baseballs and pictures of Mickey Mantle and Yogi Berra graced the walls all through the dining area. Along the walls leading to the men's room, you saw Marilyn Monroe posing with Joe DiMaggio for the camera, with the likes of Gina Lollobrigida and Sophia Loren in a stunning low-cut dinner gown. Alongside a World War II pinup of the Andrews Sisters saluting in style, wearing cute, matching military garb skits and olive-green caps, an original telephone booth remained at the far end of the bar, adorned with cartoon prints of Dagwood Bumstead and Blondie. There is an original bullet hole just above the phone with the crushed slug still intact. There is no known history about it.

The walls along the foyer side of the ladies' room had black-and-white photos of the angry women's group that tried to burn the place down, Sisters United Against Alcohol. They are portrayed wearing plain long sackcloth dresses holding signs and waving their fists. Directly over the ladies' room door was a portrait of General Patton holding his bull terrier, Tank.

The sixties contributed half-burned braziers that hung behind the bar for a few years and later taken down. Portraits of JFK, Jimmy Carter, and Ronald Regan are the last and most notable additions to the décor. Pretty much nothing changed after that for a long time.

Two booths away from where Jay is sitting, a conversation is in progress. Andy White, a retired car salesman of twenty-six years from the now-defunct House of Cars—a used car dealership—is telling a story.

"I knew this kid. See, now this is going back a few years mind you. Nevertheless, I knew this kid. He was a teenager going to school, working part time, and all that—you know, to prepare for the world. He loved the '70s Mustang. I mean, he wanted a '70s mustang more than I wanted a sharkskin suit and a new pair of Italian shoes. He would come into the lot every other day, you know. I got a kick out of this kid. He reminded me of myself a little and why I got into the car business.

"Well, anyways, every other day, here is this kid. 'Got anything?' The kid was driving me nuts. It is not like every day a car like this comes rolling into the lot, you know what I mean? I felt the kid's passion. He is stuck in this small city with this one car lot and not much to hope for, for Christ's sake. So one day, I'm out with Charlie Burns, the owner. You know who I'm talking about right? He's dead now. It was a while back, like I was saying.

"We're at this public sale in Newark. I see this 'Stang going up for auction, right? So's I bid on it for a song. It only needed minor work, so I brought it back to the lot, see, and had one of the mechanics clean it up nice. I park it in the corner of the lot where he, the kid, won't see it right away, you know. I wanted to see his reaction and all that. Sure enough, the kid comes in and spots it—*wham!*

"Man, that look was priceless. I sold it to him. I made practically nothing on it. I ate the cost of repairs. My boss Charlie thought I was nuts for what I did. But it was worth it to see that kid's face light up like that. It was purely personal. I'll tell ya, I never had any kids, a bachelor all my life. But this had to have been as close as you could get to being a father."

Jay could not help overhearing the conversation. He tilts his head toward their direction as he watches the traffic from the window. He is never one to notice cars. To him, they are a vehicle of convenience and nothing more: neither a status symbol nor a projection of alter ego—just an iron horse with lots of bells and whistles. Right now, however, he could feel what it must have been like in the era of the American automobile.

A Cadillac rolls past him, stopping for the red light, followed by an old Chevy truck. From his view, he could see a young girl on the passenger side lazily swinging her arm from the window. A gentle breeze puffs her hair, complementing a glint of reflected light coming off the frame of her sunglasses. Jay is surprised at himself that he never notices before just how beautifully animated American women are. An earthly composite of hair and makeup that are always telling a story; it's the story of magazine ads and pictorial layouts, television cinema, and movie stars.

Jason Marz suddenly embraces a sense of Americana, a kinship with his culture he never noticed before. Jay becomes aware maybe for the first time in his life that he was part of a collection of things bought and paid for that made him American and a little different from people in other parts of the world. He questions if he had missed something back in the days of his youth. He has never fussed with these machines and now noticing the metallic stallions with acute awareness, watching them as they trek along asphalt roads, built and maintained especially for them—like royalty.

The man sips his beer as his two friends sit, quietly listening. Old age brings mysterious tranquility to a tribal gathering—no one is in a hurry to speak, allowing the ghosts that trade memories time to eavesdrop.

"Yeah, he loved that car, and they sure made a good pair cruising up and down the avenue," Andy continues. "Now he is a big shot somewhere, and he drives a sedan. He grew up, and his cars grew up. And his taste in everything grew up with him. He shops out of town at some swanky dealership now, I suppose. Dropped me too. Never came back for a trade-in new car—anything. Hey, you know the difference between a porcupine and a BMW?"

His crony friends look up, a little confused by the tempo change.

"On a BMW, the pricks are on the inside. It's an old joke but still relevant." Andy lets go of a laugh.

Crony 1, still searching for closure, asks, "Hey, Andy, is there a point to this story?"

"Yeah, I'm getting to it. What I'm getting at is this. Tastes change. Everything changes. We are not all in harmony. With change, when it happens . . . do you follow? What I'm saying is, styles, diets, sometimes place we go, hobbies, movies, all that bullshit is temporary. But how do you call it when it comes to tradition, real life-changing stuff, like career, marriage, religion—we put it on like cement underwear.

"So, now, this kid grows up many times, his life changes, his cars change. He took a bite from the apple and did not want the apple anyway. So he throws it away, tries something else. Someday, a song comes on the radio that reminds him of that Mustang—the good times and the bad. The time when he had to say goodbye to youth, and if you are wise enough, you learn a lesson. That even your most honest decision turns out to be just a good idea at the time. That is all."

The man Andy contemplates for a few seconds longer.

"Edward, Eddie—that is it!" the man exclaims, slamming his fingers on the edge of the table. "That was the kid's name, Eddie Flynn. Now I remember . . . Eddie Flynn."

⚜

At 2:00 a.m., not much is going on. The subterranean nightlife of cab drivers and insomniacs is something to leave alone for most people. Felix X. Cole has a plan. He has a revelation that was eating him away. Since he last spoke with Jay, a new idea has come to him that he could not wait any longer to share. He can't remember when the germ of this all came into his thoughts because his delusions have been formulating for quite some time. In reality, Cole has forgotten things about himself that other people will never even know about. Jay Marz, his only friend, still only knows whatever Felix allows him to know; and most of that was an act.

The persona of Felix X. Cole is a clever disguise. You see, Felix Cole has a compartment in his brain that only he had access to. In it, there are plans, plans to give people freedom. Some of these plans, however, bordered on the edge of lunacy. While others are innocuous theories and thoughts, common to men of his intellectual pursuits, Felix is always able to separate compartments, knowing what was safe and what was going to land him in the looney bin. At times, he would prescribe mild mind-altering drugs to himself—his psych meds—in other instances, he would just steal the potent stuff from his mental patients.

He loads up on some common-name pharmaceuticals and knows enough about them to mix and match, without causing long-term injury or side effects. It won't be long before his Jekyll-and-Hyde game will turn into an all-blown-out tripping shindig.

At one point in the early days, he experimented with ecstasy, mollies, and old-fashioned LSD that he copped from street hoods around campus. These local party favorites to him now would be nothing more than a twelve-year-old smoking cigarettes in their parents' basement. Although Cole has somewhat of an addictive personality, he has never smoked pot or cigarettes. He is health conscious and scared to death of getting cancer.

It is a cold, dreary evening. The taxis are idling, waiting to pull in that early-morning fare. Cole walks down to the only place he knows of that still has outside public telephones that are maintained properly. He could have used a public phone in a tavern, still available at that hour, but he doesn't want to take the chance of a drunk crying to his girlfriend and tying up the line. So there he stood at the Deluxe Light Rail station in a foggy drizzle.

Cole walks past the suspicious eye of hack cabdrivers and oddballs hanging around the station. The disenfranchised always seem to eventually find a comfort zone at train stations. In the wee hours of the night like barnacles on a ship, they attach themselves to the subterranean nightlife mentioned earlier. It might be interesting to note that barnacles have no true heart—a sinus close to the esophagus does the similar function of pumping blood through a series of muscles. I doubt if they share much concern for their fellow crustaceans.

After carefully inspecting the phone receiver, Cole deposits some coins into the phone and dials the number. It was Jay Marz's number.

It rings several times before he picks it up.

In most movies, when there is a scene like this, the phone is usually right by the bed and the recipient groggily gropes for it, almost knocking to the floor. This not being the case, however, in this scenario.

Jay checks the clock, gets out of bed, and walks into the kitchen where the phone is. His feet are cold. He does not recognize the number reading from the caller ID and is about to dismiss it as a wrong number.

Or it could be an emergency, he convinces himself. *At any rate, it might be a good idea to deal with it and clear it up so they don't keep calling back.*

There is always something creepy about a phone call at two in the morning. Jay answers it with slight nervousness.

"Yeah, hello?"

"Jay? Jay, is that you?" Cole is sounding shaky.

"Yeah, Jay here. Who is this?"

"It's me, Felix," Cole answers, almost whispering.

Jay sounds a little excited. "Felix, it is two o'clock in the morning. Is everything all right?"

"Shush, shush, do not talk on the phone, Jay, this is too big. Hush-hush. Until we meet, Jay, things will be clear when we meet. Jay, today. Jay, we must meet today."

"C'mon, Felix, what's this all about? You sound like you are sweating." Jay questions.

"Hush-hush, Jay. Come to my office at ten o'clock, okay? Today at ten o'clock. Not a word on the phone. I must have your word."

Jay is getting frustrated. "You want my word about what, Felix? Not saying a word?"

"And, Jay, you must promise me—this is important, Jay—you will not let your likes or dislikes get in the way of reality." Cole's voice intensifies. "Do I have you on that, Jay? Yes yes?"

Jay is getting tired. "Okay, Felix. Ten o'clock. This better be worth it."

Jay hangs up, scratching his head, wondering why he is agreeing to this.

Why am I so easily giving in to this absurdity? he scolds himself.

Moaning, Jay goes back to bed, pulls the cover over his head, and tries to go back to sleep.

All night, thoughts of Donna haunt him as they do when he wishes she were there to shield him. He is thinking that if Donna were there, she would assure him that this is just the nonsense men do when they are without women to occupy their minds—the restlessness that drives men to bad lifestyles like the characters in Hemingway's stories.

Jay is beginning to understand what that means. By agreeing to see Felix tomorrow at ten o'clock, Jay was becoming restless and bored with himself.

Felix X. Cole hangs up the phone and walks away into the fog. He is wearing a felt fedora and a classic trench coat. He cuts a fine silhouette in the distance, opening an umbrella in classic noir style.

A cabby drinking a coffee and reading the paper watches him walk by. A police officer on patrol eyes him too. Like a stray cat, he walks into the fog with his tail in the air.

Just think about it
Lately, I've been skeptical
Silent when I would use to speak
Distant from all around me
who witness me fail and become weak
Life is overwhelming
Heavy is the head that wears the crown
I'd love to be the one to disappoint
you when I don't fall down

—"Re-Arranged," Limp Bizkit

God said to Abraham kill me a son
Abe said man you must be putting me on,
God said no. Abe' said what?
God said you can do what you want to Abe but,
The next time you see me coming you better run.
Abe said. Where you want this killing done?
God said. Take it down to Highway 61.

—"Highway 61 Revisited," Bob Dylan

From his desk, this note was handwritten on professional letterhead bearing the name of one Felix X. Cole and handed over to his secretary, Cynthia Evans, in a sealed envelope with exact instructions that in the event of his sudden demise, this envelope is delivered to Jason Marz. The message reads as follows:

October

I am a man of science and not a religious man, as you know. That being said, I believe that at least one supernatural thing has been revealed to me.

It is that God—the "Big Man" behind the curtain with a huge computer brain—has been pushing us around like chess pieces long enough. She wants me to know the truth about free will, and it is this: we are screwed!

No amount of cajoling, self-deception, acting, or false presentation will help you sneak to the front of the line to get her attention. Your best-laid philosophies and religions will continue to confuse you until now. I think that because of my lack of belief, it was that I was chosen to reveal this mystery.

Adam and Eve have known that God was a woman. The deceiver portrayed as the snake was also a woman. This could explain why the creation of Adam and Eve was such a convoluted undertaking. There is a powerful pheromone excreting externally from the female life form that is attractive to both sexes. In the days to come, I will know more.

Jesus, unfortunately—maybe a confused soul like us thrashed by a theocracy of Über women—much is being kept from him. Think of religion as a default widget. It'll disappear as soon as you add your widgets.

Until then, hush-hush,
Felix X. Cole.

This manifesto produced by Cole's worsening condition was written and completed on the evening that Cole fell into an exhausted sleep after whipping himself into a frenzy, thereby tearing apart some journals on the creation and apocalyptic literature sold to him by a homeless man.

The vagrant acquired them from a fanatic zealot preaching the end of the world. Rather than use them for his sanitary needs, he sold them to Cole for five bucks. The homeless man thought Cole was nuts. Cole, on the other hand, thought the homeless man was a harbinger of manifest destiny and believed the five-dollar fee as a test or tithe. Cole walked away smug, thinking he got one up on the gods. The homeless man stuffed the Abe Lincoln in his shirt.

While Cole was asleep, this is what he dreamed.

Dr. Cole pressed against a urinal in a large lavatory, as was the routine after finishing his business. He went to the sink and washed

his hands. An elderly restroom attendant offered him a towel to dry. Upon leaving the restroom, stepping gingerly on to the carpet, Cole was transformed into a little boy.

He was in a theater. It was a magnificent theater. The carpeting was lavish. He looked around and was enchanted by the mural work and statuary, as fine engraved plaster moldings divided the ceilings. Gargoyles and griffins adorned corners of the walls. A long, straight carpeted floor led his way. At the end of an ornate Persian carpet, his father, Abraham Cole, was there to greet him. He was dressed in a formal jacket and tie and very well groomed. He smiled with sparkling teeth. Felix never remembered him with such stunning teeth. Young Felix hurried toward him and took his hand.

Abraham Cole nodded to an usher who led them into the theater section and escorted them to their seat. Felix noticed a staircase with brass railings ascending into the balcony seats, as people gathered there waiting for the show. The lights went out, and the ceiling turned to the deepest of blue sky, with twinkling stars appearing. Stage footlights revealed a heavy velvet curtain that was about to open.

A single spotlight shines on a young girl who emerged from offstage, carrying a sign. She wore a red-and-white pinstripe jacket with red tuxedo pants and a round, white bellhop cap. She carried the sign to an easel in the middle of the stage where another girl was waiting to help her put it up.

The sign said, "Über Gals' Production."

As the curtain began to open, letters stretched across the screen that read, "An Evening in Paradise."

The pinstripe girls exited from the stage, walking in a single file to where Felix sat excitedly. The slight strawberry-blonde girl perused the crowd, spotting young Felix in the crowd where a spotlight enshrined him. Both girls now gestured to him to come with them.

Felix looked at his father, a little frightened. Abraham Cole smiled at the boy, shoving him off to go. A patron look of assurance glistened from his eye.

The pin strippers flanked Felix on either side, each taking a hand and walked him up onto the stage. As he crossed the threshold, the play began. Everything was beginning to come to life, right before his very eyes.

Felix was a man again living in the present time. He had no awareness of dreaming. Felix X. Cole was indeed in the Garden of Eden.

Eden is a very commercial-looking place. Rental signs are everywhere. Some are hand-painted; some are neon and elaborate. No one owned anything in Eden. The inhabitants are fickle, changing their minds quite often. There are many plastic fern plants and pink flamingos on the lawns. Each tiny bungalow seemed to be having a garage sale. Used items speckled the lawns. Nothing is of any value, and everything is lumped together—fur coats, tacky wig hairdos and toupee stands, etc.—with no sense of real order or tact. The only exception is the man-made trees and the nicely painted sky. Everything else is a kind of a trashy Oz. There was, however, on the other side of the Elysian river a skyline made of a huge rainbow bridge that led to heaven. Spray-painted on the side of it was a graffiti tag that said, "BE A MOTHER, NOT ANOTHER."

There were no birds or flying insects, only cherubs, and they looked like Italian paintings of little fat babies with locks of curly, brown and gold hair and rosy cheeks. They were brown, white, yellow, and pink, perfect and waxy; there may have been more, but those were all Cole could readily observe. They had an intense skin pigmentation that made them appear to radiate like colors you might find on the plumage of exotic birds or in a crayon box. Their wings, however, were much softer looking, piled in layers of the feather over feather but elaborately decorated like butterfly wings. Some had simple white parachute material like wings with graffiti tags painted on them.

Other inhabitants dressed like Christmas tree ornaments, angels, and such. It was impossible to distinguish ages; they seemed to be old souls. Cole watched them roam freely around the grounds of paradise, minding their business, talking to themselves. The inhabitants rented everything. The quality of most of the stuff went from designer labels to cheap crap. Everything seemed made in our image or vice versa.

Everyone in Eden had every gadget available to him or her, and no one was committed to anything. Things of beauty just came and went. Medication dispensers lined the street. They looked like bubblegum machines instead of parking meters. Felix felt a little high. There was no fear of losing anything or robbery because you never really cared about it, knowing that it does not matter—in plain English, to parley the verbiage of our times, "No one gave a shit about anything."

If you asked the average being on the street his or her opinion on anything, the answer would most likely be, "What do I know? God does whatever she wants anyway."

God controlled everyone—there was no free will.

While Cole was wandering around aimlessly, he found a rubber doll–like woman that was lying down in front of a white picket fence. She had a tattoo of a social media post just above her left breast that said, "No one appreciates the very special genius of your conversation as I do." On her right buttock was a mock copyright brand that reads, "Made by Goodyear." Below that was a bar code. Her latex skin was soft and supple.

Cole picked her up a carried her around with him. He eventually found a discarded shopping cart and propped her up in it. This made the journey easier. Cole studied her as he pushed his new playmate up and down the streets of paradise. Cole could not help touching her constantly. He could not keep his hands off her. It was his dream girl.

She had fiberglass angel hair that swirled around when the light went through it. Her lips were deep crimson. She never talked, which was fine with Cole. There was nothing worth saying for the average being in Eden to talk about anyway. Things were what they were, and nobody had any reason to stir the pot. Everything was attended to in a cheap, quick, commercial way.

The best thing of all is that no one feels guilty about anything, Cole mused as he fondled his rubber companion's bosom.

Everyone seemed quite happy, except for Dr. Cole. He was bored. He had a strange mental illness the others did not have; it caused him to be curious and hungry all the time. He didn't quite fit in, as if he were an alien on a strange planet.

Cole noticed in the clearing a custodian wearing a tangerine jumpsuit, occupied by throwing apples away into a large public fireplace. The custodian was humanoid in appearance but had to have been an angel of Eden disguised as a South American man that spoke broken English with an urban New Jersey accent.

Dr. Felix X. Cole asked him why he was sweeping up perfectly good apples and throwing them into the fireplace.

"Because these apples have forbidden knowledge. I burn them so no one eats them. It's the law," the man answered.

"What will happen if someone eats one?" Cole further inquired.

"They will get free will, and they won't rent stuff anymore. They will want to possess it. Then others, to keep them from changing, will have created laws. Eventually, they will have to give things up like freedom and dreams to keep what they think they wanted. First, this knowledge entices you with a promise to serve, and then it owns you. This is especially true with humans. Bad medicine, baby."

Still provoked by a symptom of his mental illness, Cole inquired, "What about love?"

The custodian looked puzzled. "Dude, that's out of my pay scale. Go ask that lady over there about love."

He pointed to a building across the road to a woman that was standing in front of easels, arranging paintings. A sign hung over the roof that read "Reptilian Galleries of Paradise."

"What is that place?" asked Cole, pointing to the building.

"It's an art gallery," replied the custodian. "There is an art in there. I can see you are from out of town. Art around here is something the free-will people do. It is completely useless, very hard to rent."

Cole thanked the custodian. He grabbed the cart and his rubber woman escort and proceeded to the gallery to find out more.

The woman gallery person had her back to him, draping a purple garland around what Cole made out to be as portraits of Elvis Presley and Oscar Wilde. These were images of both men painted with painstaking detail on stretched black velvet. Between them were a few paints by number-framed cardboard renditions of Emmet Kelly, the clown with different sad faces. There was also a fine poster collection of dogs playing billiards. The gallery lady was dressed all in black.

Cole read this to be the absence of light. It was the darkest representation of black Cole ever saw in earthly nature. The human eye never experiences pure black. (Claude Monet, father of impressionism, has taught us that what we perceive as black are absorbed hues of deep purples, blues, maroons, and greens. Only deep space or maybe hell where there is no natural light might produce an absence of reflecting lights the likes of which Cole was witnessing.)

"Excuse me," Cole said. "What is it you do here?"

The gallery lady turned to face the inquiring stranger.

"Some residences of Eden come here to look at the art," she said.

"What is that?" Felix. Cole was now pretending to be a visitor from the moon.

"It is a fake representation of life and nature here in Eden," she answered.

"Why would I want a fake reproduction of nature when I have the real thing already?"

"It's obvious," she said, almost laughing. "You fall in love with the image, silly goose."

"What? That sounds absurd. Why would anyone do that?"

"Because they ate those phony apples over there. See, the custodian is burning them. I believe you were just speaking with him. If you ate one, you would not be asking, and you would not be curious, and you certainly would not be hungry. You would understand what I mean. You would simply fall in love with the fantasy of these fake paintings. Soon you might get it into your head that you could make your own. You could bring them to me, and I would try to sell them for you, and you would starve or go insane. If you go inside, there are other paint by numbers of horses and some Venus in paradise color pencil landscapes, next to those old van Goghs over there."

"Was van Gogh here?" Cole asked inquisitively.

"Not lately," she answered. "We even have one-hundred-, five-hundred-, and thousand-piece puzzles that are completed, pieced together, glued, and framed. They are ready for hanging. Look here is one of the Last Supper."

"No thanks," said Cole. "But I might need a bathroom, if you don't mind. I'm prone to bouts with colitis, you see—irritable bowel at high altitudes."

"Here, try this apple. Then come see me again."

She handed him an apple from a pouch she kept around her waist.

Cole thought the gallery lady was very beautiful. She had short strawberry blonde, pixie-like hair, accentuating amazing fairylike eyes. Her lips were full and perfectly shaped. She wore very little makeup if any at all. Her translucent skin radiated around her black clothes. Something was tempting about her.

Trying to be cool and cosmopolitan, Cole took the apple from her and bit into it. It reminded him of a pink lady variety from the state of Washington back on earth. So vibrant were the hues—pinks, yellows, and reds—it called to mind a Cézanne still life he saw once in a book back in his college days.

He tried to call to mind all the drug-induced oblivions he ever experienced but found none to be like this. Already being exposed to free will, this feeling of vanity and worldliness he was experiencing was nothing new to him. It was, however, the supreme feeling of euphoria that enlightened him.

A supernatural state of awareness, he thought. *Nirvana—this is the birth of Venus. Its King Kong's penis, Gershwin, and porter all rolled up in one.*

According to biblical text, in the beginning or sometime soon after, when Adam and Eve lost their innocence, they realized they were naked and covered their bodies with fig leaves to avert shame. There was no mental illness in Eden at that time or addiction to pharmaceutical drugs. Mind-altering apples seemed to be the drug of choice. Exposure to the forbidden fruit had the opposite effect on Felix X. Cole. He had the overwhelming urge to shed all his clothing and run naked into the fields.

Cole and his shiny love puppet took leave of the gallery lady and ran into the Elysian field to hide behind some trees. Cole threw himself on top of the latex maiden, trying to perform one last act in this excellent place. However, it was too late.

As the intensity peaked between his temples, a blinding rage of excitement pulsated throughout his nervous system. The science behind what was happening to him was useless. He quivered and quaked, holding on as long as he could to sustain the ecstasy. He pinched his nose as though trying to hold back a sneeze. But it was too late; gusher mode was enacted.

A spent, hulking Felix X. Cole wasted the last few seconds in paradise rolling around in a dizzy fog of nocturnal omission.

He did not remember falling asleep, but when he awoke, he was in his bed. Everything was gone. The sheets were damp with viscid whitish man stuff.

Cole indeed had a new outlook on things; he did feel the magic a new religion empowered him. He went to the window and looked out over his minions. Yes indeed, he did understand everything.

Early morning
9:30 a.m.

Jay is finishing his coffee at the Mulberry Bee Hill Café, three blocks away from Felix X. Cole's office. From his seat, he could see Cole's building and floor, the very office window where he had been a week before. Although he is curious about what his friend could have wanted and what the nature of this visit could be, Jay could not help admitting to himself that he has an ulterior motive for giving in to this childishness so easily. He wanted to see Cindy Evans again.

There was something juvenile in the naughty vibes he experienced around Cindy. She would smile, and he would giggle. Cindy's attempts at being aloof just provoke him to dawdle at her every gesture like a simpleton. As difficult as it was to watch, the bus that boarded the memory of Donna has become smaller as it rolled away.

The night before, through all the tossing and turning, Donna haunted his sleep. As badly as Jay wanted to project a fresh image of her, the painting he had frozen in his memory has been slowly fading. She was becoming mechanized in synapses of his thinking habits.

There were episodes when Jay would recall to his imagination all the little scenes that he and Donna shared—self-pity movie reels of dialogue with bourbon chasers where he became the salty pirate with a parrot on his shoulder and the world pier was a long lonely waterfront quay for somnambulists and the strange. Nevertheless, despite a quick checkout form the Heartbreak Hotel, Jay knew that it was time to stop living in the past.

Jay picks up a *Fashion Q* magazine that is in the rack by a side table at the coffee shop that morning and scanned the pages. He finds photos of sharply dressed men boosting their self-esteem with tailored print sports coats and fitted shirts. It inspires him to join a gym and get in shape for spring.

He feels himself giving into that old balm again, infatuation. The cool friend of the boss who enters the office and plays the mysterious bon vivant, the unruffled bachelor. He is sure he felt vibes from her. He gives himself plenty of time today to check his look, decompose, and prepare for act II. He is wide open for any incoming subliminal flirtations. All sensors are on, and his rhetoric carefully rehearsed the night before.

Checking his watch, he has just enough time to stroll over to Cole's office. The thought of Cindy sitting at her desk acting pleasantly surprised to see him is making Jay anxious and a bit nervous. He is not even thinking of Cole at this point but the promise of finding more out about Miss Cynthia Evans.

Change the mask worn so well,
deliver us from confusion.
To find at last, in the final cast,
his face is lost in the great illusion.
Chameleon

—Rocco Bonfire

Leases

Jay stands outside of Cole's office, preparing to go in. He checks his watch and enters the building. Passing the man at the security desk, he goes to the elevator, not wanting to take the stairs and appearing perspired in front of Cindy. The doors open, and he gets on. In a few seconds, he is standing in front of Felix X. Cole's office. Adjusting his clothing and touching his hair, he turns the handle and enters.

Felix Cole is sitting in Cindy's chair, spinning around, stops, and looks directly at Jay. He holds out his hands and greets him with a loud *yeehaw!*

Not quite knowing what to make of this, Jay stands in awe, waiting for something to happen. Cole breaks the uneasy silence at last.

"Jay, Jay, punctual as usual. I knew I could count on you!" Jay says. "I knew from the other day that you were a game man. Jay, you grew up to be a real game man Yes sirree! From our first days at the university, all lines converged to this moment. You brought me the message, Jay. And I swore from that day that if any good came of it, I would share that glory with you."

Jay looks around, not sharing Cole's enthusiasm but looking for Cindy, trying not to look too lost.

"Felix, what is this all about? Where is Cindy? Where is your receptionist?"

"Oh, I gave her the day off. We need to talk."

"About?"

Felix rises from his seat and takes Jay under the arm in a fatherly way. He leads him around the room over to the window. Felix steps across him and looks directly at Jay with a deep, penetrating glare.

"Choices, my boy, choices! You see, we are hard-pressed—all of us stuck in a system of ideas out of which we have long since grown. People are sick and tired, Jay. How many styles of clothes have you gone through in your lifetime? How many shoes pens, ties, diets . . . too many, right? What works now—you see it now, don't you? A shell game. We have been a great given a gift, Jay, maybe the only true gift. It is the gift of adaption. Besides, we can do it quickly not over a billion years but faster than the speed of light. Do we not change our minds constantly? What do we do? We trade it for Freud's id, a lawless sex drive, along with egos and all sorts of viruses of the mind."

Jay steps back, but Cole being considerably taller than Jay appears menacing.

When they were younger, Cole had a habit of grabbing Jay in a headlock and swinging him around when he was excited about something. Although he has not done this for all his adult life, Jay notices it from the look in Cole's eye, hoping the same spontaneous gesture is not about to befall him.

"Felix, will you calm down? You are beginning to sound like Frankenstein."

Cole's face muscles relax. He smiles a strained smile. He does not want to lose Jay's confidence so early in the game.

"Steady, keep steady," he admonishes himself, walking around behind Jay then getting in front of him.

Jay steps back and stumbles into the chair. Cole bends over him and gets into his face.

"Listen to me, you silly little twerp. I am offering you a chance to be on the cutting edge of evolutionary change. What I am offering is not for everyone except for the enlightened ones so that they will have a chance to grow and change with their creative whimsy. I am offering a path back to the Elysian fields! I'm talking paradise, for Christ's sake!"

"Felix, please get to the point!" Jay exclaims, rubbing his temples. "My head is quaking."

"I'm talking about leasing marriages, Jay, the same way we lease everything else!" Cole unloads. "People need to be together sometimes for different reasons. What gets in the way is love, emotions, phobias, fantasy, religion. When the fever resolves itself, the healthy organism seeks replenishment from the world again. You must understand, Jay. Dig deep. Boy, there are pearls on the other end of this gestalt-ridden rainbow."

"For crying out loud, Felix, don't give me that psycho-babble bullshit," Jay counters, becoming emotional. "I know just as much about the mind as you do."

Cole, catching himself flying off the edge, reels himself back in. Calmly, he sits down before Jay like a father consoling a child.

"Quite simply, Jay, please answer me as simply and honestly as possible, all right?" Cole tries to explain. "What do you do when the apartment you rent is not working out because of unforeseen trouble. What do you do?"

"Ahh, you do not renew the lease," Jay says, playing along.

"Okay, and when the car you rented doesn't fit your new station in life, you don't despise the dealership, do you? Or your suits don't fit anymore because your fat ass is loaded with donuts—is it your tailor's fault?" Cole is struggling to hold on to his last nerve ending.

His voice is beginning to escalate, but he catches himself again and lulls back to a steady calm.

"So when the high school sweetheart doesn't want to play house anymore or you just decide one day you want to dress up as Zorro and play the ukulele in Macy's window at high noon . . ."

A look of sudden insight flushes over Jay's face. He has just started listening and is realizing that Felix Cole is revealing a creative side of himself of which Jay never thought he was ever capable.

Just how preposterous this plot sounds, Jay is thinking. *Am I the butt of some joke?*

However, still following its simple lines, the naked logic of it is something Jay himself might have even felt many times over but unable to tap into.

Suddenly, Jay feels like the student in school understanding an algebraic equation for the first time and feeling very special about it. He is unable to stop the plan from unraveling off his newfound tongue.

"Yes! Yes! You just let the lease run out!" Jay concurs. "Under the terms of the contract, that is in the best interest of both parties. People can go on without any hard feelings."

Cole shoots him a look of excelsior.

"You are getting it, my boy!"

Jay is almost on fire now.

"And if you love someone with all your heart, what better way to say it than to lease for, say, umm, twenty years," Jay mumbles.

Cole is about to shit himself.

"Or one hundred! Would someone go out on a limb like that if they did not have to? This will replace the golden ring, my boy."

It is a decisive moment. It is the bullfighter looking into the eye of his worthy adversary.

Cole takes to a flight of fancy as he begins waltzing around the room, pretending to be evading a bull as he continues.

"It could only be love that is powerful enough to issue such a commitment. We would have eliminated the bullshit clause—the liar's, the cheaters, and the frauds. No ridiculous swear-ins such as 'til death do we part' or 'love, honor, and serve' issues. You are locked into the terms of the agreement, and they are negotiable. Therefore, there will be no need for broken hearts because the bullshitters will get out of the game at the first sign of commitment. As a marriage counselor, Jay, you should understand this better than anyone."

"I'm thinking, Felix, less nervous breakdowns, bankruptcies, alcoholism . . . well, they might be replaced with happy drunks. But still, nothing being perfect, I think it could work," Jay adds.

Cole begins to sing and dance around the room to some kind of victory song he is singing. He reaches into the desk drawer, pulls out a bottle of bourbon and two glasses, pours equal measures of the magic elixir, and hands one over to Jay.

Half smiling and still looking out the window, Jay takes a swig.

"You know, Felix, you could be on to something," Jay says, turning the glass between his fingers and looking over at Cole. "A little tweaking here and there—a few adjustments, maybe some fine-print clauses, a few carefully crafted addendums—and this could work."

"I have some things to set up, Jay. I have to arrange for lawyers," Cole seals the deal, now smiling. "Do not do anything or breathe a word to anyone. Only contact me from a secured phone. No computers or emails. If people hate you, Jay, just remember they hated me first."

This last statement causes Jay to wonder for the first time if Cole is not suffering from mild megalomania or if he is just a frustrated, burnt-out, tired hack like himself, ready to try something different and new. The idea of going out on their own with a fresh idea might be good for the both of them.

Just look at him, Jay thinks. *Stuck in a rut. Poor Cole. His clothes are bad. His hair is pathetic. Standing there staring into space. His ear hair is out of control, with no one to tell him it needs trimming. And that cologne . . . ah! The crummy stuff we wore in college. Crap. It didn't work then, and it isn't going to work now to improve the poor bastard's social life. Moreover, what about poor Cindy? Trapped in this office all day inhaling that rotten scent . . . ah, Cindy! Yes, I now have an excuse to talk to her. Bingo!*

As the inspirational thought of Cynthia Evans slips into Jay's mind, it triggers a new battery of questioning for Dr. Felix X. Cole.

"One question, Felix," Jay breaks the contemplative silence. "What about love, religion, guilt, and all of that? Why wouldn't people just live together?"

Cole's face broadened into a toothy smile.

"That is the beauty of it, Jay. We could set up escrow accounts for our clients, an added security so no one feels jilted or taken advantage of. This is a special service we provide and stand by so no one is left in the cold when the winds of change come. One-stop shopping. No fuss, no muss, bring your nuptials to us."

"The winds of change, Felix? Felix, what is love? Now answer carefully, my friend. The future of my decision could depend on how you answer this."

Jay sits back, taking a deep swig of his bourbon. He could feel the subtle sensations of alcohol running through his circulatory system like little firefighters rushing to put out a brush fire in his frontal lobe.

Let's see how old Cole handles this, Jay muses, up Cole. *A confirmed bachelor, no ladies' man by anyone's standard, not a romantic, not gay— zero social life, unless you count those crummy lectures. What do I know about my old pal, Felix X. Cole? I don't know anything about him. The truth is, he is so damn boring I never realized I do not know anything about him. Besides, somehow he is my only close friend.*

Cole turns from the window and appears to be in complete control of his senses. Not looking at Jay but looking through him, not looking around the room but looking past it—Cole has taken on a persona of a confident businessperson and a mystic. He reminds Jay of the amusement park when he was a kid. There were coins they gave out on the carousel ride, a silver coin that had a comedy and tragedy on opposite sides.

Cole could not have been more possessed as he answered.

"The path to love lies in knowing how to master the eyes, the ears, the masculine, and the feminine. It is a path. For those who choose it, there is no final destination and, therefore, no satisfying explanation about its end. Oh, folks who want to follow convention can still do so, Jay. Our demographic is for people way out of the traditional box anyway. We are neither infringing on tradition, nor do we want to. We are an alternative. We are offering a way back to the Garden of Eden."

Jay awakes the following morning, rubbing the residue of alcohol-induced sleep from his tired red eyes. He gets out of bed and goes into the kitchen to pour a glass of milk. He takes a seat next to the window and peers into the street. The adjacent tenements provide a major impact on his viewing experience. The everyman cinema presents Mrs. Smith watering her window plants, and college girls putting their laundry out to dry on the fire escape. Down below, pedestrians walk their dogs while the town crier walks around with newspapers in his hand.

Jay measures the pulse beat in his temples—sometimes fast and sometimes slower—while comparing it to the rhythms of the sidewalk traffic. There is a spiritual momentum to it all, even moral at times as Mrs. Smith tends her simple window garden. The motion seizes up at the girl draping sweatpants and T-shirts over the fire escape ladder, providing for a different reality to taper in. Nature imitates art when you place characters into a landscape; a different relationship develops.

It must have been Cole's reference to the Garden of Eden that hit a nerve with Jay. Somewhere in a cloudy, dense arrangement of dark thoughts and self-denials, Donna's premature departure, and the unsettled business with time and future rattled something deep inside of him.

It was not fair—Donna, who has always been his ideal, the iconic soul mate, companion in paradise here on earth, suddenly cut down on the street. Permanently removed from Jay's life in a senseless unrelated act of doom, preserving her in eternal youth. Donna has petrified into a still-life image trapped in amber for time immemorial while Jay is left behind to grow old in a dying dimension.

Cole unwittingly challenged Jay during that obtuse phone conversation the other night to confront an issue that Jay has been running from since Donna's death—"What will you do when the winds of change come?"

For the first time since Donna's demise, Jay is at a crossroads. He must distinguish who is living and who is dead. Jay will always see Donna forever in paradise wearing a flower that never fades; she will always be as young and as radiant as the photo on his shelf. Death has done that for her. However, he can also envision Jason Marz growing old by a tree and eventually dying.

Will we have ever endured growing old together? Jay asks himself. *Could we handle the quantum weight of thoughts that occur, creating a silence that permeates the car during resentful outings or pretending to read magazines at the doctor's office? What of the gross familiarity couples endure with each other under the guise of what our parents called love, honor, and serve?*

Are we so vain as a culture to think that the vast lessons—tried and tested for generations, embedded into our traditions so brilliantly by our elders—are nothing more than nature's trick to keep the planet populated with humans? How can the fleeting ideals of youth challenge the wisdom of the ages and win? Youth is a temporary condition. The young are always growing older. The wisdom of the ages was always old and stays that way.

It is hard to grow old, Jay muses. *But it is harder to watch the ones you love to grow old and not be a part of it. Donna will never be old.*

Like those two crazy kids in the garden, on that lost day, we will only know the beginnings of things.

The phone is ringing. Lost in two parts hungover and one part self-pity, Jay allows the phone to ring, unable to force himself to answer it.

The answering machine comes on with its dull greeting, the beep, and then from a speaker no bigger than a dime, out the angels come:

"Hello, this message if for Jay Marz. This is Cindy from Dr. Cole's office . . ."

PART II

A Conversation at Bruce's Roost

"I always liked cars. I don't know, maybe it's a guy thing, but to me, everything seems to revolve around the American automobile. I love those old movies with gangsters in those heavy Fords, the surfer guys throwing their boards into an old beat-up woody. There is something American about it . . . a romance no one talks about anymore. Movie stars in convertibles and all that . . . man, I don't know how I ever got into this stock-and-bond thing. I am a car sales representative at heart. I guess white-collar crime is the closest I'm gonna get to be a real gangster. Ha!

"I'm getting out, Shelly, starting new. Taking whatever is mine out of that market and launching my dealership right over there in that broken-down parking lot. I got my first car there, don't you know, The House of Cars? Man oh man, what a beauty—a '70s Mustang, burnt orange. It needed some work. Did all the remodeling myself. Learned a lot about cars taking that Ford apart. I got a good deal on it.

"I mean, could you imagine Humphrey Bogart stepping out of a Renault or how about Lauren Bacall or Kate Hepburn leaning against a Volkswagen with those tapered dresses and high heels? Now there are no real facts to prove this, what I am about to tell you—and it is more of just my opinion—but I believe that cars of a certain era were designed with the idea of a woman's shape in mind. I mean—follow me on this—it is the natural inclination for a man to like two things the same way, cars and women. So why not build automobiles to accommodate a woman's fancy. I mean, many women like to dress up, right?

"The way I see it, if I was a girl—I mean, who would want to get in and out of a car that's going to wrinkle your dress or rip a stocking, right? I'm just sayin'. Not to mention the make out potential. What could be hotter than making out in a big, old Buick? I would always see these guys around by the stock exchange with those little, skinny expensive cars, and it used to drive me nuts. The girls they liked were the same way, skinny long-legged things. No pun intended, ha-ha! Before all this status-symbol mucky muck, cars were just plain cool. Yes siree, baby doll. The American automobile was just a part of everything, I remember growing up.

"One time my father told me a story. He was getting up to go to work, and he used to get up real early before the sun came up sometimes. Right? So he gets into his car, this chunk, big, ol' Chevy. I remember it had this V-shaped hood ornament thingy, cool as balls. Anyway, he gets into his car, see, and starts her up. Suddenly he feels this hand on his shoulder, and his blood ran cold. He is thinking he's gonna get robbed or something, right? Well, it turns out, it was his brother Charlie, my uncle. Uncle Charlie's wife was always throwing him out of the house. He had nowhere to go, so he climbs into my old man's car to get out of the cold and falls asleep. Those back seats were like trampolines. My dad was always hollering at me for jumping around back there when I was a kid. Yeah, that is what I am saying. Well, anyways, the American automobile of the 1900s—whatever—a kind of personal fantasy to me I just don't want to grow out of it."

Shelly Connolly flips her electric cigarette and blows a puff of vape steam just over Eddie Flynn's head. She fidgets back, uncrossing her legs so she can pull herself closer to the table. Shelly rests her chin on the palm of her hand with exaggerated interest as she studies the contour of Eddie's handsome face. The overhead lighting spirals through the smoky darkness, accentuating the drama of his chiseled features.

"Boy, oh boy, I never heard anyone make selling cars sound so sexy," Shelly purrs.

"Besides, I am a natural salesman," Eddie chimes.

They share an infectious giggle as Shelly takes the conversation and a sip from her Chambord-and-champagne cocktail.

"Well, in my trade, there is not that much salesmanship involved. The product pretty much speaks for itself. What you see is what you get, with full disclosure on any extras. We can change the subject, if you want, I don't want to spoil the party."

"No, do go on. I like you, Shelly. Tell me more."

"You learn a lot in this business," Shelly continues. "You learn about people, sex, love, and money. Besides, if you are honest with it, you learn more about yourself than anybody can reveal to you. I could never confuse sex and love. Love is a hard drug.

"So sex—I suppose it is a few beers and a bourbon chaser away?" Eddie jokes.

"Well, almost," Shelly continues. "You see, what they never really understood about us courtesans is, for the most part, we are not jealous of anyone and we don't hoard for ourselves. What we offer is the housewife's secret—that something extra that you can't get at home. We are the genie in the bottle. The housewife and the girl next door want to keep power and rightfully so, and that power is right here."

Shelly gestures with a halfhearted crotch grab.

"If things get out of hand, the whole balance of nature could turn over. Think about the fall of great empires of the past. Take Greece, Rome, or any other ancient society, for example. Invading armies did not bring them down—it was decadence, the plain overindulgence into everything they could not have. As soon as you tell someone they cannot have something or you can have all of this but not that, the next thing you know, there is a fence being built around the taboo. That's according to the gossip I hear, anyway."

Shelly touches her hair, adjusts her clothing, and bats her false eyelashes—an automatic tick brought out by unconscious conditioning.

"The power, as I refer to it as, should grant us almost religious sovereignty," Shelly goes on. "We are mentioned in the Bible on numerous instances as harlots, whores, strumpets—whatever. We are not traveling salespeople. Clients come to us. One of the problems is, so many women abuse their power. It's not always loving, but they go through the matrimony ritual and act out the scenes just the same. People continue using the word *love* too many times, under pretenses. It loses its magic. Some use marriage as a stepping-stone or a status enhancer. It is a way of 'starring out,' as my friend Heather used to say.

"Now great ladies, on the other hand, they go far above and beyond for their spouse—often unappreciated, I might add. They do not need to rely on the age-old myth of sex. The women I admire are strong. They make things happen, important things. Like families. They instinctively know what is important in life. They are not silly about their secret. They do not want to share it with the chambermaid. And they stand up to a man who is a bum. Since you brought her up, Katharine Hepburn in *The African Queen*, I always wanted to be that kind of woman."

"I see it all the time in the way men choose cars," Eddie responds. "It is all up to what you value. Someone once said, 'You can't cheat an honest man.' Arm decorations take many forms."

The expression on Eddy's face crystallizes to a sensitive seriousness, almost a little boy's quality of self-consciousness—a trait that betrays him when he acts calm, cool, and collected. It is a type of tell that he cannot help, like blushing or nervous laughter. It has always been a dead giveaway to his sensitive side.

Although he has always thought of it as a weakness and tried to hide it whenever possible by employing humor or heavy-handed machismo, Shelly always saw through it and plays it like a fiddle, sometimes making him squirm or just watching him play out the scene, secretly admiring how adorable she thought Eddie could be when the flaunting boy plays.

"My mother told me a great truth," Shelly continues. "Do you want to hear it?"

"Go, you are doing well, baby," Eddie says.

"She said, 'Pay attention to how a man treats a waitress because in six months, that is how is going to treat you.'"

"That is interesting," he said.

"The judges and the clergy—they work so hard to come up with philosophies and legislature to protect the American voters and salvation," Shelly goes on. "Even though politicians are our highest-paying clientele. Nevertheless, the clandestine agreement is what they are after."

Eddie shakes the last bent smoke from his box of cigarettes and lights it. He draws a long drag and pushes the smoke away from his face.

"What about the whole procreation side of it?" he asks. "We are breeders, aren't we? Somebody has to keep this party going."

"Yes," she answers with a matter-of-fact eagerness.

Shelly gets excited and straightens herself on the chair, waving a bit of smoke away as if to see Eddie more clearly.

"Children are our prodigy, as they say. That being said, Eddie, I am so glad you went there. In my opinion, childbearing is the most precious part of love. If people could realize love naturally, they could be more honest with their consequences."

"I need a drink."

Eddie signals over to the waitress and orders a vodka martini. Shelly has another Chambord-and-champagne cocktail.

Eddie is getting uncomfortable with their talk about love and its attributes.

He was married for almost ten years to a woman he realized he did not love six months after he married her. He was young, naïve, and engrossed in the role he was playing as an aspiring powerbroker. Caught up in the image of his time, he never completely blamed Vanessa; she was playing the role too. They never had kids. They were children themselves from a generation that was much too selfish. Children would mean choosing between expensive hotels on a private beach or Disney World and an expensive diamond cocktail ring or converting their bar and entertainment salon into a baby room. Vanessa was not having it; besides, Eddie always had the feeling that if he did not keep feeding the monkey, she would step out on him. He was right.

He suspected Vanessa of cheating and/or excessive flirting on more than a few occasions. The truth was, they had both overstayed a visit that should have been a temporary station on a youthful journey through life; however, the paperwork and binding contracts in an adult world consider tokens of affection as costly investments and valuable possessions to be doled out accordingly. Vanessa could take him for everything. Eddie was beginning to question, at the budding age of thirty-three, what exactly everything was.

"You mean, more honest than love?" Eddie asks.

A page has turned in the conversation. Shelly has taken to a faraway look. She abandons her e-cigarette and pulls a tobacco stick from her bag. Not wanting to draw attention to the subtle mood swing, Eddie attempts to veer away from the topic. But it was too late.

"Yes. Sex and love are not the same thing most mature people would agree with," Shelly breaks in. "So why don't folks be more careful when choosing?"

"Choosing what?" Eddie ventures in, simply unable to resist.

"The altar to which they choose to pray—be it the altar in their heart or the one between someone's legs. Can you pass me that ashtray, please? Thanks."

Shelly's hardened professional exterior was melting down. She is emoting, unfolding to Eddie. She has been since they first met two years ago.

It was a spring day, about two years prior. Shelly—born and branded Michelle Bridgegate—was new in town, having just moved in from Baltimore where she was a promising art student and emerging artist in her own right.

She had come away from a broken home. She stayed with her mother who was a recovering alcoholic. Her father, Danny Bridgegate, was a degenerate gambler who left the family high and dry and ran off with a girlfriend when Michelle was twelve. Her mother, Anne, eventually remarried a man she had met through a counseling group some years later.

Shelly's stepfather, Tom Agist, had lost his wife to a ruptured aneurism that killed her instantly. Tom and Jenny Agist had only one child together, a very troubled boy named Billy. Billy had the right combination of defective genes to one day land him squarely into the wheelhouse of crime and debauchery. His problems were compounded with drug abuse and bipolar episodes; it was only a matter of time that he started approaching young Shelly inappropriately.

One evening while Shelly was home alone working on her school assignments, Billy came home and began verbally abusing her. When she attempted to leave to avoid his advances, he got violent and raped her. He later died that night of a drug overdose. Shelly always believed it was suicide.

Shelly never told her mother of the rape because although Billy was a sadistic, selfish, troubled kid, his father Tom was a very nice man with a heart of gold who made her mother very happy. Her mom got a long-awaited miracle for a second chance, and Shelly was very happy for her. Shelly left home to embark on her career in the arts, taking her secret with her and a letter from the clinic informing her she was pregnant.

At the train platform, everyone smiled, wishing her luck with hugs and kisses. Shelly thought that she might never see her mother again. Shelly left something else to rot and fester on that tearful afternoon, a severed slice of self-esteem.

After having arrived in a new city—alone, broke, depressed, and pregnant—she took a job as an artist model at an art and media university. The pay was not that good. She became part of the university staff that allowed her to continue classes free. The flexible hours enabled her to supplement her income by working part time at night and late afternoons as an exotic dancer at a gentlemen's club called Bruce's Roost.

One night while performing her routine, she passed out on the stage and was immediately brought to the emergency ward of City of Friends Medical. A very elegant Hindu doctor with comforting large, dark eyes dressed in a partial sari of flowing cotton and beautiful design appeared before her as an angel while she peacefully awoke from her seizure, informing Shelly that she had lost the baby.

After a brief stay at a women's shelter and some rough encounters with the reality of being penniless, destitute, and fundamentally alone, she decided to find some charitable strangers who could help her.

In its early history, Bruce's Roost—or, The Roost, as it was called—at that time was a notorious gay bar. The owner in those days was one of the city's first openly gay businessmen to come out of the closet named Marty Balaclava. He was a transplant from Chicago. Marty Balaclava was a journalist who started an underground newspaper called *The Paradise Lost and Found* that he independently ran and distributed. The witty stories and event calendars he published for his isolated group provided a venue for a community that had no voice in the area. His popularity grew.

When the opportunity arose to invest in a vacated structure on the edge of town and convert it into a nightclub, he took it.

Because of The Roost's transient location, situated close to a train station and a major highway, it was accessible for "out-of-towners" who wanted to keep the anonymity and a low profile. Patrons would be able to visit it with impunity.

Originally Marty wanted a quiet, classy bar where gay men could meet and greet and share some conversation and attitude adjustment after a long week of work. But business partners had a different plan bringing in their crowd with a dubious agenda. The dead presidents and hard cash flow from a lucrative drug trade soon began rolling in, bringing along with its motorcycle cavalcades and bare-chested men in leather vests and jackboots.

The club specialized in theme nights and all-night, dress-up disco parties that ranged from drunken bacchanals to drug orgies. Some special-access bathrooms were equipped with glory holes. In all fairness, there was one stall designated for handicapped patrons. The cellar was converted to a members'-only fight club; for a yearly membership, the boys could punch the living hell out of each other or just watch someone get pulverized over beer and pretzels.

There was seldom any trouble outside the premises so the local police left them alone. The location was offset outside the perimeters of residential neighborhoods, but the local folks never really knew what was going on there.

The club ownership and any future designs on its tone and manner slowly began slipping from Marty's control into the hands of part owners Jackie Frye and Frank Church who eventually pushed Marty Balaclava out. Jackie and Frank continued to run The Roost into the ground.

Things began to spiral out of control when undercover narcotics agents were busting people on a whole host of illegal activities. It wasn't until some local politicians were exposed in graft and corruption charges that the stories exploded outside and news media got involved, and it was becoming just too juicy for the press to cover up. The Roost eventually folded. Everyone involved went to Jail, except Marty who was living comfortably in Miami.

Under new ownership, the property once again flourished under Giamatti Developers and Sanitation. They rebuilt it and cleaned it up free—a community service they provided for all the fine local folk in town who use their services. It has since become a local watering hole and gentlemen's club for some of the stockbrokers and financial crowd. The girls were pretty the drinks were cheap, and, as long as the tips were sizable, everybody was happy.

Eddie and Shelly became friends, which was unusual, considering the profile of this type of crowd. Although it considered itself a gentlemen's club, a gentleman was the furthest thing you would find there. Nevertheless, being an amateur escort and not a very good one, Shelly conjoined with Eddie, a second-rate bond broker with no talent for it, who was married to a spoiled shrew and locked into a thirty-year, fixed at 12 percent mortgage, no kids, and a new car. He is condemned to a slow death that pretty much sealed his fate through a bad marriage for at least four more decades or until someone reaches the finish line of "'til death do us part." Eddie found solace, however, in bringing Shelly lunch and coffee.

These little friendly outings have been slowly becoming a routine for almost a year. Eddie met Shelly quite serendipitously. It was raining, and Shelly was coming out of a used bookstore called The Backward Scholar with an armful of parcels, dropping her things all over. Eddie offered her a ride, and the rest was history.

It started innocently enough, with casual hellos and salutations then light banter; now they are becoming soul mates and saving a fortune on a personal analyst. The relationship had always been platonic; however, recently, Shelly had been teetering on the edge of getting personal and was wondering if Eddie was aware of it also.

Meanwhile, back at Bruce's Roost, Shelly is slowly getting drunk.

"I am just a regular girl deep inside. I mean, listen, I can't speak for gay people, all right? But they fall in love, have sex, and get jealous too. Nevertheless, we all have to react to outside stuff just the same, no matter who we are. Rights, guilt, laws, and families—too much stuff gets in the way. Like I said sex is easy. Love is hard."

"Shelly, in this light you look like a Picasso painting and just as hard to figure out."

Now getting a little tipsy from the Chambord-and-champagne cocktails, Shelly changes the subject.

"Did you know that at one time I was an artist model? I was so shy, I would never pose nude. None of the artists would use me. I broke the inhibition by becoming a stripper. And then after realizing my true talent, well, here I am—escort, courtesan, lady of the evening."

"So what about your art?" Eddie asks.

"Oh, I didn't know you were such an art enthusiast, Edward. Sometimes you are more like a mental ward instead of an Ed *ward*. Waiter, another one of these please."

Eddie casts a look at her, trying to reference where that absurd comment came from. The timber of Shelly's voice is escalating into singsong.

"What about my art, you ask? Well, a funny thing happened to me on the way to art class."

The waiter brings Shelly's drink, and she drinks it in two gulps. Eddy tries to slow her down, but it is no use. She was on a tear.

"Shelly, let's get out here," Eddie says. "C'mon, you're not yourself tonight. We'll get something to eat at the diner."

"Eddie, it's time for a moment of truth," Shelly says teasingly as she looks up at him sideways, a little drunker than before. "You know I am a hooker, right?" I'm sure you must have had some parental guidance somewhere in your wonderful life of cars and comic books that warned you about us."

Eddie washes down his drink and watches Shelly try to pull herself together. Eddie knows she is not much of a drinker. He has never seen her drunk; he has never seen her drink, except for bottled water or coffee. He tries to figure if she is really getting drunk or just dramatizing a good buzz. He has a slight premonition of where she might be going with this. He begins to challenge her.

"First of all," Eddie says, "you are not a hooker. You are an escort, and they are not the same, I don't think. You say you are a hooker and a courtesan and all this because you think it is cool to sound like that, but you wouldn't know hooking from a hole in your ass."

"I would so. Well, whatever," she says. "Has anyone ever warned you about us?"

"No, clue me in," he says.

"We make bad dates and only good for one-night stands."

"Correct me if I am wrong," Eddie went on, getting a little drunk himself, "but the whole idea of escorts implies a date, does it not? Besides, have you forgotten I am aspiring to become a vintage car salesman? The only difference between purpose and us for all intents is four wheels and an oil change. I have to seduce customers into buying my product too."

Eddie is now starting to feel the numbing cotton-head dullness between his ears of the vodka martinis.

"A used car salesman, huh? And a married one to boot. Eddie, do yourself a favor and rent me. It is easier."

She drops her head for a split second as a brief glimpse of vulnerability came across her face, just long enough for Eddie to read it.

"I'm only asking about dinner. I haven't had a decent meal all day." He is beginning to slur.

"Okay, but I warn you. I will not sleep with you on the first date."

"Oh! How sweet. You're not *that* kind of girl. I will make sure to get you home early, in case mom waits up."

Shelly starts giggling and then, out of an alcohol-induced reaction, starts laughing. She reaches out and grabs Eddie's hands. He now begins to laugh as they bring their heads closer together; almost banging heads, they met in the middle for a soft landing. Eddie is resting his forehead on Shelly's scalp.

"You know, Eddie, a girl—the kind whose momma would wait up—she could fall for someone like you," Shelly gently whispers, her chin tucked into her chest.

With that, they pull away.

Shelly sits up and springs back and then, bringing her face in close again, looks Eddie straight in the eyes. She points a disciplinary finger at him.

"Are you hitting on me? I should slap your face," she says, jokingly exaggerates a mock slap.

Eddie parries it, laughing.

They both fall back to neutral corners and just look at each other. Eddie orders a drink. Shelly declines the offer.

"I do have a rule that I have never broken," Shelly slurs. "I never get personal with local married guys. It could get messy. I hate messy. In case I forget, remind me, won't you?"

"If you are going to make me your babysitter, okay!" Eddie answers. "But if you misbehave, I'll tell your mom."

Shelly laughs, holding on to the table.

"What's so funny?" he asks.

"You! You, you . . . jerk."

Now he is laughing too. As the laughing subsides, Eddie can notice that Shelly is whimpering in between her heaving sighs, mascara trails running down her cheek. Locks of hair are falling across her face. As she tries to wipe the running mascara from her cheek, it messily gets on her hand, creating a bigger mess. It is not just the booze, Eddie senses—it's something else. Something emotional is hurting Shelly.

"Excuse me. I have to go to the ladies' room."

Shelly gets up and meanders to the restroom, allowing Eddie a moment to reflect on what is happening. Whatever it is, he is not focusing on going home but completely absorbed with Shelly and how girly girl she becomes when she drinks the cuteness out of her wit.

The past conversation is a blur of details:

Did I ask her out? Did she just tell me off? Am I too incoherent to get it? Am I being stupid? All these insecurities are spinning around Eddie's head like a schoolboy on his first date. *What am I talking about?*

He let his mind go blank for a few seconds that seemed like hours. A song came on the overhead speakers, and it triggered something in his head about an orange Mustang, a local girlfriend from high school, the open window, and her wispy wonderland of hair of perfumed smells and soft flaxen edges.

The waiter brought another drink.

God bless Andy White, Eddie muses. *I never even went back for an oil change. When too much time passes between people, it is easy to just forget about them. Andy was a good guy. He looked out for me. I am a real piece of shit.*

Shelly comes back to the table, uneasy and drunk.

"I just got sick in the restroom. Eddie, can you take me home?"

Eddie snaps out of his reverie.

"Of course, but we will have to take a cab. I can't drive like this."

Eddie has the waiter call them a cab as Shelly leans against Eddie.

They go outside to wait. It had been raining but has then reduced to a drizzle. Pedestrians are walking along with umbrellas and holding papers over their heads. When the taxi comes, they get in.

Shelly opens the window and lets the cool misty rain splash her face. Eddie thinks about old Andy White for a moment, then turns his attention to Shelly.

The Taxi pulled up to Shelly's apartment. Eddie helps her up the steps. He takes Shelly's keys and opens the door.

Eddie is amazed to see how the other half lived, the soft mind-twizzling effect of a girl who lives alone. There is nothing like it to a man who has forgotten the charms of a sensuous woman. The wonderful scent of vanilla and orange permeate the air. Shelly throws her bag on a chair, excusing herself, disappearing into the bathroom.

Shelly's apartment is an eclectic collection of Oriental pieces that told stories. Ornamented carved soapstone figures impress on tables. A four-panel screen with mother of pearl inlays and chinoiserie designs depict winding villages and gentle songbirds. Figurines and knickknacks adorn shelves. Oil paintings of floral arrangements and simple nudes sketched and finished in charcoal and Conte chalk cover the walls. Each work bears a signature in delicate script on the lower corner—Michele Bridgegate.

A soft couch, a TV, a compact audio player, and a throw rug complete the ensemble. Colorful scarves and loose clothing are flung around. Eddie is careful to check for any clues that there might have been a male companion around recently, like maybe a boyfriend of a lover, but not a clue of one masculine object of interest. Eddie is getting nervous. He has not an inkling of what to expect.

The bathroom door slowly swings open, and Shelly appears in her pajamas. They are white flannel, with little cats and dogs chasing each other, up and down, causing a stripe pattern. She is barefoot.

Shelly is standing in front of Eddie and rubs her eyes. Her makeup is all cleaned off, and she presents herself to him, completely unrehearsed, smiling gently and sleepily, still feeling the effects from the Chambord and champagne.

"Thank you, Eddie," Shelly says.

"For what? I think that is the obvious thing to ask." He lets go of an awkward laugh.

"For the evening. For being a Gentleman."

"That's easy, Shelly. It is amazingly simple when you care for someone.

Eddie has no idea where these words are coming from as it poured out of him. And he knows he could not have made them up on the spot if he wanted to.

"What is so simple, being honest?"

"You see, Shell, I'm figuring it out," Eddie continues. "Romance is a byproduct of true feelings. That's why they can't teach it in school. You stumble on true feelings along the way, alongside the path of bullshit, sort of like good and evil. Something moves you to something you are unfamiliar with, and you react. It is never clear because there is no road map. But somehow, the other person understands it too, and then like déjà vu or something, you know."

"Synchronicity?" Shelly answers.

"Yes, thank you. What was I saying?"

"C'mon, Eddie, get some lead in your pencil and straighten out your Longfellow."

They both laugh.

Eddie leads Shelly to the bed and pulls down the sheets. Shelly climbs in as Eddie tucks her in.

"Good night. Will I see you again?" asks Eddie

"Same time, same place," answers Shelly.

"You are going to have a headache tomorrow."

"I know. We'll meet on the next day."

Eddy lets himself out and does not go home. He sleeps in his car. He left his wife that night, and he quit his job. Now he owns a vintage car dealership and lives happily ever after.

Shelly is painting images of nature again and raising their children.

Some days have passed. Jason Marz and Cynthia have been busy ironing out the details for Cole's new business venture. Jason has arranged to keep his old office still functioning on a part-time basis, enabling him to still help his steady clients until he could work things out with Cole. The new agency will not be as demanding as the marriage counseling, Cynthia could handle most of the paperwork, and some portion of it could be transferred to Jason's secretary who will maintain her regular hours and work from home on projects that would mostly entail calling clients and sending forms. All related materials would be delegated to specific agencies in charge of handling technical problems.

Yes, this seems to be a win-win situation, and Felix X. Cole could not be happier.

The last few weeks have left Cole a blur of activity as he jettisons from office to office, meeting with attorneys and paralegals who are executing and formulating the contracts and conditions. He is working relentlessly with preparers, making sure the terms of the leases could be bulletproof and binding under the courts. Whatever was not altogether Kosher, he pushed through anyway; after all, he is on a mission from the proprietor of paradise.

He meets with partners in the financial industries who could explain and prepare escrows and terms. As the variables and conditions expanded, more interested parties became involved. Unhappy heads of the clergy, social groups, and secular strongholds, along with their lawyers to be met with, were put on hold, if not ignored altogether. Cole organized a marketing group to test the waters and gauge which demographic would be most interested in a social product of this kind. The results were astounding. There were more people on the fringe of social norms than to be expected, a silent minority that was growing quickly during the overall cultural demise.

History has shown that when cultures are in flux, there are gaping holes left unattended in the fabric of great mosaics. Felix Cole is on his way, not to mention that their venture is costing a small fortune. But with the help of banks and private investors that latched on to the radical view and effects, with such a concept presented, a huge social paradigm shift was about to tsunami.

Jay and Cindy have become somewhat of an item since they agreed to meet a few weeks back. What started as a stylus agenda to get things going and establish business meetings slowly procured into long lunches and afternoon outings.

During this whole undertaking, Cole is virtually invisible. Jay only contacts Felix by outside the phone to a secured number he has established with the phone service. Any other messages to Jay were through direct communiqué via Cynthia Evans, his secretary to the head of personnel.

Late autumn was morphing into early winter, leaves were indeed swirling, and the sky was picking up the periwinkle hues of November. Jay and Cindy are walking in the park during one of their extended lunches, trying to find a hot dog wagon. Most of the seasonal vendors, however, have packed up for the winter season and gone south, not unlike the great flocks of geese that have left the ponds deserted and abandoned, except for some playful gulls.

They decide to sit by a playground that was still intact, and Cindy rests on a swing. Jay tosses around some ideas in jest, coming up with comical names for the new agency.

"No muss no fuss, bring your nuptials to us," he says, bringing a chuckle to Cindy's rosy cheeks.

Her scarf is tightly wound around her neck, barely exposing her face.

They stroll over to the pond that was silvery from the overhead sky and skipped stones. Cindy searches her pocket for a coin and tosses a penny for good luck, as is tradition. Each ripple in the water casts a ring of melancholy grays and murky greens. A brisk wind rose from the pond and blew through the buttons of Cindy's coat, causing her to shiver. Jay notices the slight tremble, takes her into his arms, and offers a warm embrace. It meets no resistance.

As they slowly come out of a soulful hug, Cindy opens her eyes to notices just behind Jay's shoulder an elderly man. He is looking across the pond through a pair of binoculars. He could not have been more than five feet away.

She taps Jay's shoulder and whispers in his ear, "Don't look now, but we are being watched."

"Really? By who?" Jay asks.

Cindy pushes her right hand between their chins and extends a pointed finger in the direction behind him. Jay suddenly is experiencing that uncomfortable feeling one gets when you are crowded on a park bench by the only other person in the entire park.

Jay slowly turns his head, pivoting his body in a half twist, finding himself looking sideways into the stylishly mustached face of John Pittsford, a retired professional bartender and bird watcher.

"So sorry, I didn't mean to surprise you. But there is a pair of bufflehead sea ducks that fly in from the Antarctic this time of year then fly back just before spring. They usually fly in groups, but these two must have separated from the flock. They are male and female."

"Which is which?" Cindy asks, suddenly becoming very intrigued.

"Oh, well, you see the adult male over there . . . the males are black-and-white plumage, with iridescent green-and-purple heads and a large white patch behind the eye," the birder says. "They have marvelous golden eyes, by the way. Females are grey toned, with a smaller white patch behind the eye and a light underside. You see how they dive. Watch how the one who gets the plankton first shares it with its mate."

All three of them watch as the male bufflehead dips below the surface to retrieve a tender morsel of krill. When it came back up, it did indeed deposit it into its mate's wanting beak.

"You see! Did you see that?" shrieked the excited old man. "This is the only angle on the whole pond I can get this point of view. Here, would you like to look?"

John Pittsford gestures to hand the binoculars to Cindy, still encapsulated in Jason's arms. Cindy takes them clumsily and holds them to her eyes.

"Oh, Jay, this is amazing! They do have golden eyes."

"Yep, see? I told ya so! Pretty neat, huh?"

Being forced to let go of Cindy, Jay takes the glasses from her to have a look. Although he is less enthusiastic than his company, Jay observes out of courtesy more than interest. After a brief look, he hands the binoculars back to Mr. Pittsford, who continued sprawling as if Jay and Cindy were not even present, not to mention having stampeded on their first groundbreaking kiss.

"There is a woman that comes by here a few times a week with bags of birdseed, and she feeds the birds all winter long. It is a little late in the day for her now. The police give her real hard time. Last week she and another woman who was helping her unloaded two huge bags of feed and thistle into the pond . . . they wheeled them over in a cart. You should have seen it. The whole pond was wild with so many different birds flapping and squawking. What a remarkable sight. She changes her feeding times to throw the police off their game. It works pretty well, but the birds must think she is mad as a hatter."

Mr. Pittsford lets go of an infectious chuckle, causing Jay and Cindy to laugh along.

"With all the fine warnings and all, she still sneaks back. See, all the gulls come around the pigeons too. They wait for her now. They see people here, and they think it might be her. Isn't that something how they know to do that?"

There is not much more for them to talk about so Mr. Pittsford bid them goodbye, trekking to the other side of the pond in pursuit of the "Birdfeeder Lady," his partner in crime. Jay and Cindy watch cormorants posing on a rock, wings extended, while the bufflehead dined in exile.

There is a cure for being alone too long, and it is in a kiss. Cindy looks up from her huddled stance and meets Jay's eyes intimately for the first time without saying a word. The sun pierces Jay's iris in such a way that caused golden flecks of pigment to encircle his pupil.

Now bonded in an unspoken experience of that, kiss they walk hand in hand for the rest of the day.

The Second Delirium of
One Felix X. Cole; or:
The Collective Consciousness
of Carl Jung

The sun was setting earlier. It was evening, but the overcast sky and persistent misty rain made it seem much later. The roads, however, were still moderately congested with rush-hour traffic, and the slippery road conditions made the commute much more dangerous.

The intermediate traffic lights and commuters turning off the road to get home were making him nervous. He veered off the highway and took a route that was not at all familiar to him. He knew, however, that it would put him on the back roads.

Sometimes, during precarious weather like that day, Felix would tempt fate and do dangerous things. He once shut off his lights during a blinding rain, relying on the scant lighting from the streetlamps to illuminate the white lines separating him from oncoming traffic. On a straightaway, for example, he might remove his hands from the steering wheel and massage his penis to see if he could achieve an erection before the car lost control. That night, however, he was just driving at unusually high speeds on the back roads of industrial outposts, slamming over potholes and uneven paving. The residue of psychotropic drugs that were corroding various parts of his brain was dormant for a while.

For the last two weeks, Cole was working like a machine, completely sober, sane, and cognizant of his surroundings. He conducted his business deals brilliantly. He swayed public opinion and convinced hardcore financial people that his marketing plan to lease marriages was an idea whose time has come. He presented his arguments flawlessly, assuring all from the private sector to the academia that this was not only an alternative lifestyle and posed no threat whatsoever to the standing traditional norms of matrimony.

But not unlike the generals and physicists working on the Manhattan Project and Yucca Flat, Felix Cole himself was not sure what he was about to unleash on young Sue and Johnny Doe—or himself, for that matter.

Cole headed north along a filthy stretch of old bridges and truck-servicing centers. The night got darker as the rain began to come down in steady pellets. Cole stopped for a red light. He looked into his rearview mirror and noticed three figures were sitting in his back seat.

At first, he was frightened, unable to move. Then the slow, warm dementia of his reasoning began to take over. He carefully observed. He immediately noticed they had pasty-white Caucasian heads and hands with segmented arms and legs. Cole's first bout with reasoning was that aliens were abducting him.

It was a longtime interest of Cole's to study alien-abduction stories. As a teen, he loved the tabloid stories in the back pages of *The True Confession* rags. No UFO story was worth its salt if not reported from a remote, off-the-beaten-path location. It was only logical that superior beings might want to study him. He suspected for some time that they were watching him.

Cole recalled hearing about it when he was a young boy and the news of Betty and Barney Hill was all over the tabloids nursing a population that was already being weaned on comic book superheroes and B-movie matinee idols.

It was shortly before midnight on September 19, 1961, when Betty and Barney Hill had the experience, which was to shape all modern alien folklore. They were driving from Canada to Portsmouth, New Hampshire. Near the resort of Indian Head, New Hampshire, they stopped their car in the middle of Route 3 to observe a strange light moving through in the sky. The next thing they knew, they were about thirty-five miles further along on their trip and several hours had elapsed.

To Cole, this was showtime. He studied their look in his rearview mirror but did speak.

On the sides of their heads were red boxes with a circle inside divided by a design of black-and-yellow triangles. Their eyes were just blank and expressionless orbs. They looked exactly like crash-test dummies.

They did not speak, but Cole did not worry as he could feel a communication, an intuitive sense that rocked his senses. Visions of St. Paul being knocked from his horse and struck blind flooded his mind. In nanoseconds, Charlton Heston was kneeling before the burning bush. Stanley Kubrick was conducting the Viennese waltz. Unable to translate the rapid-fire succession of cartoon imagery, Cole would later recognize it as the collective conscience that Carl Jung wrote about but Cole could never quite understand. But now that he was experiencing it, *holy moly!*—it was a mystic experience; at the very least, a religious experience of a broader category, not induced as the result of deliberate practice but proof that he was tempered by fate's crucible and chosen to walk with the gods.

"What do you want from me?" Cole screamed out in a high-pitched animated voice, wanting to communicate with them. "Am I going to die?"

Besides, to that question, an overpowering need to defecate came over him. His irritable bowel syndrome came on him like a tidal wave. He felt the weakness of all of humankind in his bowels. He sensed immediately a great failure. That was the damnation of Adam—the wall that divided humanity from the glory of paradise was two bucket seats and a console.

Nestled in the back seat of Cole's Lexus was a family of aliens from parts unknown that are going to show him the way. It would not be so easy to go with them; much will be expected, and much will be required of him. As any mortal gifted with a mission at the decisive moment, Cole would have to overcome tremendous self-doubt.

"To be in the presence of divine intervention and to suddenly have to shit your brains out is surely a sign of unworthiness," he confided to himself.

He continued speeding down the highway. The scenery that engulfed him was a horrible, grotesque industrial nightmare. Tires and wooden pallets were stacked in front of sooty buildings. Barbed wire fences surrounded the yards deposited with mountains of car parts and rusted steel piled up to the sky. The only audible sound was the humming of his automobile engine and a junkyard dog barking. Abandoned gasoline pumps with greasy handles displayed analog digit counters with black-and-white numerals.

Texaco signs shed light on to the highway, as deep puddles of oil and rain overflowed on to the road. Green workman's clothes with gloves and visor caps were piled in corners of the lots next to old chairs that were left outside. "Ring and Valve Specials," "Oil Changes," and "Free Tire Rotations" squealed from the marquee like carnival barkers ghastly illuminated by a single stained yellowish spotlight.

Dimly lit garages with a coating of tobacco-brown wash that oozed over everything became runny in the misty rain. A steady pillar of smoke and steam rose from the truck stops like the whole damn place was ready to heave. Coal tar vapors from cresol seeping out of wooden boxes and telephone poles filled the air, bringing a wave of slight chemical nausea to Cole's distraught digestive system. It was a living museum of Esso signs and Sunoco ads.

A big, orange neon Gulf sign shone like a harvest moon across the highway, besides a vintage tiger clinching its fist, inviting phantom motorists to "put a tiger in your tank."

Cole had to make a decision.

He turned into an eatery called The Blue Diamond.

The big blaring sign overhead read:

OPEN 24 HOURS: HOME OF THE FOOT-LONG HOT DOG
AND POP FRANK'S FAMOUS CHILI

The Blue Diamond

Cole parked the car, securing his visitors inside. Hurrying as quickly as he could, he walked briskly through the doors, trying to look as normal as possible.

Over the years, The Blue Diamond had done little to retain its original charm. If not for the sake of inspection and code violations, only a little more than an occasional paint job or loose hanging telephone wires would change. The Blue Diamond was sparsely crowded most parts of the day, with pasty cadaver-like patrons and crusty old men sipping coffee while brooding over racing forms and sports pages.

Transparent ocher tints of yellow bled through the walls, coalescing with the poor lighting from overhead fluorescent lamps. The combination creates a sulfur-like texture that affected any object in the room, transforming them into a faded yellowish black-and-white photo. Deep blue and pearly white tiles were the hallmark of The Blue Diamond, back in its heyday. Many tiles replaced over the years with different grades of stock due to the unavailability of the original tile. When it became an unattended act of neglect issue altogether, the blank spaces caused by missing tiles and broken panels remained, exposing the skeletal grout-and-mortar properties that are the nostalgic remains of The Blue Diamond.

Back in the day of beatniks, hippies, and drag-car racing, The Blue Diamond was the hotbed of activity. Kids came from all around to hang out in metallic speckled-blue vinyl booths and played the tableside jukebox. The culture was more circumscriptive when Pop Frank first took it over in '64.

One of the more metropolitan aspects of The Blue Diamond was that in the men's room—a cramped tiny room with two urinals and a stall with a sink and mirror—was a collection of coin vending machines. They were dispensers for cologne so a young man could freshen up before going back to his booth to chat with the ladies and smell like his father. Next to that, for the exact change, you could get a Flex comb that would bend in your pocket. It was made of new durable plastic and basic black—not like your father's hard, brittle tiger-stripe brown Bakelite pocket comb. That type always had missing teeth because they snapped easily. Finally, yet importantly, were tiny decks of playing cards with topless divas on the face of the cards. These were images of women who were beauties of unbridled imagination, standing in high heels or sitting on cabana beach chairs, some waving umbrellas or sporting sailor hats worn on top of fluffs and bundles of bouncy curls, redheads blondes, and brunettes— white women of no discriminate age all flashing their perky breasts and bloomers.

In 1964, television broadcasting consisted of only a few network stations, and that was controlled at home by Dad. Places like The Blue Diamond offered a venue for an emerging genre of a new demographic—the aging teenager.

About a decade or so before The Blue Diamond came into existence, teenagers, through no fault of their own, were on the brink of a new identity; they became recognized as young men and young women. By the time Pop Frank and The Blue Diamond came along, the teenage persona was becoming a pseudo adult with its brand of distinction, its own music culture, and food. An industry of absurd foodstuffs came on to the scene, solely to assure the teenager a rightful place in society. Besides, due to the moral majority restrictions still in place on American society at that time, prohibiting decent women to show you their breasts, The Blue Diamond and other truck-stop diners across America provided vending machines with playing cards featuring topless women. Supply and demand and the American Way.

The aging teenager, however, would soon have to move on and either somewhat conform and get a job or get married or become an artist, beatnik, hippie, or vintage car enthusiast.

Given the number of junkyards and mechanic garages that lined the street around The Blue Diamond, car enthusiasts could get parts cheap then show off their souped-up cars on Saturday-night drag races. The off-the-beaten-path location and a long straightaway unhampered by traffic and traffic lights made it the perfect drag site venue.

The rusted skeletons of old Pontiac GTOs and Firebird classics still cluttered the garages around The Blue Diamond. As it stands now, mostly octogenarian teenagers gather there to wax nostalgic over a cup of coffee and Pop Frank's chili.

Unknown to Felix X. Cole, directly across town headed west, about four traffic lights, was the used bookshop The Backward Scholar where Shelly Connolly would visit to buy art books.

Four blocks past there going into midtown was the lot where the now-defunct car dealership, Little House of Cars, was before becoming an empty parking lot—just about the time young Eddie Flynn first met with Andy White who found him his first Mustang.

Not any of these people at that time had an inkling that free will was going to play such a significant part in changing their lives.

Upon arriving at The Blue Diamond, Cole avoided eye contact and walked directly back to the men's room. His colon was on fire. He flung the door open, entered the stall, unbuckled his trousers as quickly as possible, let fly his pants to his ankles, and began to evacuate.

Holding his head in his cupped hands, he was hoping the alien dummies would not be there waiting for him if and when he should return to his car.

What is this all about? he wondered.

A feeling of euphoric relief rushed through his thighs. He felt numbness in his feet as a feeling of well-being came over him.

Lifting his head from a crouched position, he read a poem written in graffiti script lettering with a felt marker on the door facing him:

> Hourly, I sigh,
> for all things are
> leaflike and cloudlike.
> Flowerily, I die,
> for all things are
> grief-like and shroud-like.
>
> —D. Thomas

And next to it, someone wrote in florescent blue letters on a hot-pink background, decorated with party designs of ribbons and sparkles along a border of cupcakes and candles, which reads:

> If you sprinkle
> when you tinkle,
> be a sweetie
> and wipe the
> seatie
>
> —Rocco Bonfire

Cole knew that he must decode this prophecy.

He was brought to this strange place, led to this exact stall, made to encounter the highlighted dancing letters, the crash-test dummies...

Yes! I almost forgot about the visitors in my car. Why else was I brought here to this place? What is the purpose of this horrific shit that is draining me of precious energy? Three aliens in the car. Three coins in a fountain, each one bringing happiness. Too many coincidences, Cole thought. *Of course, they could not get me out of my car any other way except to attack my bowels. This had to be the collective consciousness of Carl Jung at work.*

Cole cleaned up and pulled himself together, rushing out of the stall in frenzy. An old man wearing a NASCAR hat was waiting outside the stall to get in and use the facilities.

Dr. Felix X. Cole greeted the old man, all happy and weird exclaiming, "It's all there. The prophecy is in there!"

He pointed to the stall as he ranted.

Cole ran to the door and left The Blue Diamond. A server leaning against the counter shot him a look of suspicion.

While Cole was outside fumbling with the keys, one of the kitchen help having a cigarette also observed his strange behavior. Before opening the door, Cole looked through the window on the passenger side. He then got on his knees and searched under the car. They were gone. The three visitors were gone.

He then opened the door and sat straight back rigid, staring into the rearview mirror for quite some time without blinking before starting the car.

The old man in the men's room waved his hand to clear away the odor of stench and foul decay. He searched the stall for a cryptic message. The only graffiti was the following:

For the Best Blow Job in Diaspora County:

Call 555-555-XXXX

The old man wrote the number on the back of his matchbook.

An excerpt from a Felix Cole's journal:

November

In Eden, everything is all right.
The inhabitants are kept stupid while the fruit of the
tree of knowledge knows everything.

Well then, why doesn't the tree tell the people what to do?

Why? I will tell you why.

Because it is a proven fact that evolution provided us with saws and *brawn*, giving us an out to cut them down.

Therefore, my message today is this: In this world of godlike technology where processors and microchips are electrocuting reptilian brains faster than the speed of light, have no fear. You can always throw your fucking computer into your old man's swimming pool.

The sign painter with his steady hand applies a finishing stroke of paint to the door. It is an old-fashioned office door of heavy oak. The glass window is opaque smoky gray, like the office doors in noir detective novels. The door lever is a smooth brass handle affixed to an ornately gilded plate. It was custom built to Cole's specifications, along with the hand-painted lettering that displays the company name:

MARRIAGE ARRANGEMENTS AND NUPTIAL AGREEMENTS PREPARED

DR. FELIX X. COLE AND JASON MARZ, LLC,

MARRIAGE COUNSELING AND JUSTICE OF THE PEACE

Jay is standing outside the door, holding coffee and donuts, admiring the work. The painter slowly moves to step aside, opening the door to make way for Jay to enter. The office has been officially opened for one week; due to some last-minute furnishing plans and inconsistencies in Cole's scheduling, a slight delay kept the cadre from taking any appointments, although the phone was ringing off the hook. Many people were interested in the avant-garde establishment that was occupying the third floor of the very hip and trendy Lyceum Building.

Cindy is sitting at her desk, already busy going over the appointment schedules and paperwork that is accumulating before her when Jay comes into the room. She has a look of slight preponderance, brow furrowed with eyes squinting in concentration, as she reads from notes she has taken over the last few days. Storm clouds are usually an ominous sign of foul weather, so it is also when female intuition sends an early-warning sign of hunches, up and down their spine. Some unsettling patterns are forming:

"A man with three wives, and they are all cousins . . ."

"Hello, I have an unusual request . . ."

"Hi, umm, well, my boyfriend . . . ah, well, partner sort of . . . ah, can I make an appointment? And do you guys farm out to referrals?"

"Good morning, Ms. Everett," Jay burst in, smiling. "Where would you like me to put the coffee and donuts? Since we are not seeing anyone as of yet, we may as well start our day with a traditional morning pastime as we pretend to be a normal business. Has anyone heard lately from our good Dr. Cole?"

"Well, aren't you a sweetheart?"

Cindy cleared some things from the desk and prepared a space for their snack.

"He called and will be in shortly with the game plan. Jay, I have something for you."

She went to a desk drawer and pulled out a T-shirt. It was plain white with sexy lettering:

No Fuss, No Muss, Bring Your Nuptials to Us

Cindy stood up and posed with it across her chest, presenting it to Jay.

"I got this made up for you. I have one for Felix also. What do ya think?"

"I love it. Let's get some made for our clients."

"A little tacky, but I love it too."

She giggled in an irresistible tone, part valley girl and part naughty rasp.

"Speaking of our clients, Jay, have you gone over any of these applicants? There are some things that—"

The phone rings, and Cindy leans in to answer. With all the brevity of an astute office worker, she handles the information, jots some notes, and professionally truncates the call.

Jay looks on, sipping his coffee to wash down the last bite of a glazed twisted cruller. Cindy looks stern for a moment and then mentions to Jay.

"That was the *Community Conscience Chronicle*," Cindy begins. "They would like to interview with you guys. I have been getting calls like this all week. How do these organizations know who we are so quickly?"

"Who knows? They have spiders and search engines all over the place. Cole is probably up to something. What did you want to tell me about the applicants?"

Without a knock, the door swings open, and man and women are standing in the office, silently looking at Jay and Cindy. Cindy immediately greets them, telling them they need to make an appointment.

The man was a swarthy, slender youth of medium height and dark color. He wore a beige cotton shirt with a vest and poorly fit trousers. His hair was longish and unattended to. He had a slight beard, sparse in places and not fully developed as is fitting to a person of his age, being somewhere south of seventeen to twenty-one.

The woman who appeared much older was Latin American and Chinese. Her eyes bore the characteristics of Cantonese origin, with sculpted cheekbones so prominent you could slice cheese on them. Her lips were pulled tight as if hiding botched dental work. She had a petite frame and short-cropped hair. There was a slight impairment in her walk as they loomed toward Jay's, arm in arm, to introduce themselves.

The woman began speaking first. She introduced the young man as Abdul, a foreign-exchange student attending the community college on Court Street. The woman's name was Jeni, or Jenny, a second-generation American citizen from parts unknown she never said where from. They want to be married—but only long enough for Abdul to obtain citizenship, and then they want to terminate it. Jeni will obtain an agreed amount of twenty thousand dollars, paid by Abdul's family, for her participation. They saw the ad for "no muss, no fuss" nuptials in a restaurant window and came over.

"This might be more complicated than you think," Jay said. "Can you call and make an appointment? we will discuss options. You might need an attorney's advice on some issues."

Jeni begins to snap her gum and become belligerent; Abdul begins to panic and starts looking around nervously. He starts telling Jeni he wants to return to his country. Jeni is now ranting at Abdul, accusing him of bullshitting her.

Cindy notices a protruding baby belly on the woman as she stood profile, pointing her finger and cursing at Abdul. She nudged Jay to look in the direction of her impregnated paunch, and it became clear that the woman did not want to lose the twenty grand. Jay advises them to return in a day or two when the office remodeling is complete. Cindy pens in an appointment on the back of a business card and hands it to the woman.

They leave, murmuring down the hall. Jay notices them leaving from the office window as they shuffle from the building and walk across the street, melding and folding into the scenic urban mix.

Jay is beginning to get the same hunch that Cindy is already feeling. Something is brewing. Cindy lifts her head and holds some papers for Jay to read. She is studying Jay over the last few minutes.

She knew there was something to talk about. Something is not right. The mystery is in Cole's recent behavior and obscurity, his absenteeism and lack of accountability—too many things moving quickly, getting done without communication. It is almost as if there were a secret agenda to which Jay and Cindy are not privy.

The way Cole has been pulling off this whole caper from the get-go has all the earmarks of a well-planned conspiracy. It is almost as if Cole is trying to make a public statement and using the weakness of public morality to make his point.

A page from the news desk of Wallace Sinclair, writer for the *Lennox News Breakfront*:

> Some north-side residents say a local business is threatening to destroy the traditional values of a community by imposing a secular program into an already faltering, weak and morally bankrupt community

system. According to recent polls, the business will soon be booming for a local firm that leases marriages.

According to sources, the offices of Dr. Felix X. Cole and partner Jason Marz have filed with the local and state bureaus and the chamber of commerce for licensing permitting them to structure and lease time-shares of our most coveted sacrament. If allowed to do so, this will be the first endeavor of its kind to allow persons to either renew vows at the end of the leasing term or get out of the commitment legally, without any of the traditional fallout that is usually associated with a divorce. Dr. Felix X. Cole, the mastermind of this start-up, is quoted as saying to our own Byram Smith who caught up with Dr. Cole as he was leaving a local diner, "No muss, no fuss, leave your nuptials to us," before scooting away in a taxi.

Uptown News:

A follow-up tonight on a story we first told you about…

Unrelated article:

The police have arrested an unemployed homeless man for yesterday's robbery of the Washington Pickle factory. His bizarre T-shirt identified him. He said the celebrity entrepreneur, Felix X. Cole, gave it to him. Founder of No Muss, No Fuss Nups.

Felix Cole was popping up all over the place. There were sightings of him making phone calls by the railroad tracks and locals reported seeing him at The Blue Diamond, a landmark restaurant here in town.

He was everywhere he was supposed to be, except at his office where Jay and Cindy were holding down the fort waiting for the prodigal son to come home.

Back at the office, Jay is going over one phone call after the other. It was a flow of unadulterated hedonisms.

Jay is scratching his head when Cindy came up behind him and gently began massaging his neck and shoulders.

"Cindy, what are we going to do about this one?" he asks.

There was a curious couple of an older woman and a younger man. She, Daria, wants to retain him, Cal, as a sex toy. However, she must have him appear wanting to marry her to show her estranged husband that she too can be desirable enough to a younger lover. It is important that she appears desirable enough so that he, Cal, would be willing to marry her on the merit of her "sensual prowess" alone.

This would allow her to act out a revenge ploy that would bring Cal into a joint business venture that Daria and her estranged husband share, thus crippling his relationship with his bimbo secretary and other girlfriends who have been benefiting from the windfalls of Daria's hard work and commitment to the successful chain of haute couture boutiques.

These were the creation of Daria's late husband Rolland Chase who died one snowy night in a mysterious plane crash, coincidently six months before her involvement with current hubby.

As a bonus, she needs to be showing off Cal, the nubile acquaintance, at the country club and other social venues while retaining the option to get out of the relationship when her overactive vaginal mesh reaches its saturation point. He, of course, will agree to go away quietly. There will be an agreed amount when the time comes at the end of the lease. No muss no fuss—next!

A man with three wives and they are all cousins.

As these scenes are all flashing through Jay's head in rapid succession, a look of numbness comes over his face.

Cindy stops rubbing Jay's neck and comes around in front of him.

She gently takes the papers from him, saying, "Jay, we have to talk."

The phone rings. It is Karen Mitchel—Jay's secretary from the counseling office.

"Mr. Marz, there are all these reporters here and church people representatives," Ms. Mitchell informs. "They have been coming around all day. What do you want me to do?"

"Close the office, Karen," Jay says. "Tell them I am out of town and go home. I'll call you. Thanks."

"Are you okay, Mr. Marz? Anything you want me to do?"

"Just get home safe."

They hang up.

Cindy is looking out the window. Down below, the streets are filling up with pedestrians and bottleneck traffic. Trucks are idling outside in front of the building.

A news van just pulls up. A woman of about thirty-five steps out of the van, dressed in smart-business outfit, holding a microphone. The crew is hovering around her, adjusting her clothing, and propping her hair.

A youthful middle-aged man is lugging a large video camera on his shoulder, giving her direction. There seems to be a protester of some sort waving a sign, illegible from their height. Cindy twists and turns to see what is going on.

There is something about a mob that makes people want to join in. Even from the safety of a fourth-floor office window, Cindy has the desire to be a part of it on the street. Maybe it is the anonymity, the feeling of knowing that the focus is not on you but in an anonymous way it is all about you. However, being the focal point and isolated in an office that is not easily accessible, your vulnerability can transform to sheer fright.

These sets of emotions all coagulate when Cindy thought she spotted Felix Cole, pushing his way through the zombielike hordes that were tugging at him. It was then she gasped and reached for Jay.

"Jay, do you know anything about this crowd? Is the mayor making a speech or something?"

"No, we are not even supposed to be open for business for another week."

"Have you spoken to Felix recently?"

"No. You know I haven't. No one has. The last time we spoke, he said he has it all under control . . . Oh shit! Look, there's Cole, he's outside arguing with some reporters! He just grabbed someone's camera and threw it on the ground. People are pushing and shoving. What we are going to do? This is not good!"

Byram Smith is an old-school muckraker and the poison pen of the Lennox News Break Front, LNBF. He is intuitive and sharp, but most of all, he has an inferiority complex brought on by a misshapen forearm and hand caused by his mother's ingestion of thalidomide during her pregnancy with him during the sixties. Thalidomide, the drug taken by pregnant women in the late 1950s as a remedy for nausea, was thought to have inhibited the development of new blood vessels at a crucial stage in the pregnancy, causing deformities of arms legs and limbs.

After his first encounter with Felix X. Cole and the cool dismissal, Byram Smith has a vendetta. He did some follow-up work on Cole that led him to the Lyceum Building. Some hotbeds of information and undercurrents of good media frenzy were already brewing; Byram Smith was there to turn up the heat.

He went around to local community centers and well-known rabble-rousers to get them to help stoke coals, and then he just sat back leaning on the Breakfront News car, holding his notebook and pen, carefully taking notes with his overly compensated left hand that he trained himself to use. His penmanship was excellent. All through high school and college, Byram Smith always excelled in penmanship. He was also the fastest and most accurate typist in the newsroom. He never seemed to sleep and never missed an opportunity to exploit. If the natural course of nature was slowing him down, it was not below him to bend the rules of ethics to get one up on his competitors and move the story along.

Byram Smith did not like Felix X. Cole. He kept a black book spreadsheet of prominent names, from local politicians to colorful publicity seekers, and kept dossiers on the whereabouts and happenings of potential news breakers. His instincts were twenty-twenty. His tiny apartment walls are filled with framed articles of his conquests. His nickname around the office is "The Ninja."

Cole has just left his apartment. He hails a taxi and is on his way to meet Jay at the new office. Cole took special measures to groom that day. His hair is in place and his shoes are polished. He looks every bit the privileged character he thought himself to be.

The taxi driver alerts him that there was some kind of traffic jam ahead. Cole has the driver leave him off three blocks before the Lyceum Building so he could walk to his new office, in hope of bypassing any minor obstruction the local flotsam and jetsam were bound to create.

As he got closer, he notices people carrying signs. One sign said, "No Muss, No Fuss—Keep Your filthy Hands off Our Nups."

Cole begins to realize that the protester and newspeople are there to find him. As he gets closer, he could see the Lyceum security guard holding some newsmen at bay. No one at that point knew what Cole or Jay looked like, so Cole is able to make his way to the door, pushing and squeezing by.

All was going well until reporter Byram Smith from the Lennox News Break Front recognizes him, and then it became pell-mell disorderly.

Cole begins pushing and ranting like a madman. The shouts and obscenities are inaudible. Cole's ranting becomes a ring of sound inside a ringing cymbal. Cole grabs a woman's papers and rips them up, throwing them into the crowd. He then grabs someone's tie and pulls him down.

He is alertly recognized by the security guard who helps him escape the melee and escorts him into the building. The security guard locks the door behind him.

Cole exchanges some small talk with the guard and exits the lobby through the stairwell entrance. He holds tightly to the banister, catching his breath. A bead of sweat forms just under his hairline. He notices a reflection of himself coming off the safety glass panel storing a fire extinguisher. His eyes are wide and panic stricken. His neatly coiffed toupee is now off to one side, exposing clumps of original discolored hair from beneath its cover.

It's over now. Cole is at the tipping point. The kettle is about to boil.

Cole is panting as he runs up the steps as fast as he can. The dull roar of a mob is echoing on the floors below him as he stops to catch his breath. As he reaches the fourth-floor landing, he is sweating profusely. He flings open the door and runs down the hall to the office. Pushing on the new handle, he tries in vain to open the door.

Cindy and Jay hear the racket. Jay lets him in as Cindy still watches the crowd; some newspeople have already entered the building.

Felix X. Cole enters the office in full composure. He walks around, greeting Jay and Cindy as though he was in heaven and everything was all right.

Jay and Cindy are transfixed by his madness. Unable to speak, Cindy just looks at him, frozen. Jay, on the other hand, still recognizes him as his old pal Felix but can't help thinking this is another stunt.

"Felix, are you okay? Where have you been? Felix, what is going on?"

Sgt. Timothy Barnes of the District 5 police stations are enjoying a quiet routine night at headquarters. In his drab office, a few community photos and citation plaques hang in disarray. Packages of cookies and some coffee and stained folders clutter his desk. The only exciting highlight of the day was that of a shoplifter being apprehended at Walt's Camera and TV for putting a five-finger discount to some CDs.

Sergeant Barnes is going over a surveillance tape when the dispatch came through. The burn voice of a police dispatch unit squelches through the three-inch speaker of his police radio: "A group of people is illegally gathered in front of the Lyceum Building, brandishing posters and banners. Not clear what the issue is."

Looking over the report, he dispatches some units and decides to go out there and check it out personally. Little does he know that by the time he will get there, Felix X. Cole, a prominent pillar of the community and staunch supporter of the policemen's ball, would be getting escorted into the big Mariah, laced up in a straitjacket.

Jay stands in disbelief at Cole's maniacal appearance. Cindy's eyes are as wide as silver-dollar pancakes, unable to blink as she watches Felix. Cole captures the room with his air of confidence and an assertive catwalk. A mass of hair tilts on his head to one side like a thespian fedora. Slight beads of sweat trickle down the sides of his face. His eyelashes look as though they were made up for the stage.

"Jay, this is wonderful! The office is packed," Commander Dori speaks. "We are doing it, Jay. This is a great success! Look at them, and everyone is talking. I just overheard a pair of twins about to mate with a government scientist—"

"Felix, I can't do this anymore," Jay interrupts his monologue.

A look of discontent melts over Cole's face. It is not what he wanted to hear but was to be expected, despite his efforts to play down the calamity that was unfolding. A distorted twist comes over Cole's face. Cole looks like a disappointed child after learning his parents are lying to him about Santa Claus.

"What are you talking about? You can't give up now. We are just getting started! Jason, I received another message. I wasn't going to tell you until later, but we are on our way to great discovery. This is big, Jay, bigger than us."

Jay just shakes his head in disbelief at what he is hearing.

"We? Us? I don't want anything to do with this," Jay responds, incredulous. "I have to get out of here. You, these people, this room—everything is nuts! Does anyone know we are doing this? Are we filed with anyone? I think you made this all up, Felix. These licenses are all bogus. They will never hold up in court. You are crazy, Felix—gonzo-wild delusional! I don't know how I let you talk me into this. Cindy comes with me. We are getting out of here. Don't try to stop us, Felix. The police have already been alerted, I'm sure."

Jay runs to the window like a panicked child and begins banging on it, yelling for help. Cindy runs to his side, comforting him.

Felix X. Cole crouches like a lion and roars, his mane hanging off the side of his head. Eyebrows furrowed, he is controlled anger, pushing his words through clenched teeth.

"Are you quitting, Jay? I won't let you quit," Cole says, seething. "Sit down and shut up before I throw you out of that goddamned window. You are out of control, Jason. Your homeostasis is breaking down, out of whack. Remember when you said you wanted to help people get what they want? Happiness, no guilt, all that mumbo jumbo about freeing everyone from the shackles of too many restraints? We are breaking the rules, Jay! Now you want to change your mind. I won't let you. I will not tell you."

In a failed leap, Cole stumbles over himself and scrambles to the floor. He crawls to Jay, grabbing him around the legs, still grimacing and pushing exhausted air through tightly clamped jaws.

"I won't let you leave!" he growls wildly.

Having lost the mobility of his legs, Jay grabs on to the desk so as not to be pulled on to the floor—safe from Cole's clutches where Cole might choke him to death. Cole is almost climbing him like a rope.

"Dr. Cole, stop!" Cindy yells, calling to Cole. "Please, you are hurting him!"

"Hurt him?" answers Cole. "I'll break the little bastard's legs!"

"Cindy, get security! Downstairs! Call 911," Jay screams to Cindy.

Out of panic, Cindy jumps on Cole's back, locking her legs around his ribs in piggyback position, locking her ankles around his girth, securing him around the neck. Cole loosens his grip on Jay as his toupee slides forward over his left eye, temporarily distracting him.

The unmistakable wail of a police siren, then two, catches everyone's attention, bringing them to a standstill. A different-sounding, eerie distress signal cuts through the room, bringing everyone's awareness to full focus. A security guard making his rounds checking the floors has observed the melee on the fourth floor and called 911.

Jay is now pulling himself over to the window, watching the police below. Officers are entering the building. Still mounted on Cole's back, Cindy could see over his shoulder. An ambulance has just arrived on the scene.

All three just watched through the window in silence.

"Oh shit! The police are coming in, what is going on?" Cindy asks as she descends from Cole's back.

"It's a mob, Jay!" Cole cries out frantically, panting, lunging toward the door. "They are pissed off. They want to burn us at the stake! Someone told the media what we are doing, and they are trying to foil our plans. Don't let them take me, Jay, they must not succeed!"

Cole runs to the door and dashes into the hallway. He breaks the emergency fire extinguisher glass door and takes the extinguisher into his arms, bringing it to the office. Once back inside, he locks the door and pushes the desk against it. Jay and Cindy watch on in disbelief.

Jay cautiously comes around to Cole who is staring at the door, clutching on to the extinguisher so intensely he is white-knuckled.

Outside, the police are confronted by a daisy chain of protesters that are comprised of Cole supporters, most of which are his patients, former patients, and sympathizers of the cause. They are waving signs that say "The Happy-Go-Lucky Lollygaggers."

This new group that has emerged on the scene was until recently a quiet social gathering of assorted oddballs that came together once a month under the organization and tutelage of Felix X. Cole. It started as a kind of social workshop for the socially impaired. They carried signs that declared their manifesto under the name of HGLL. Felix X. Cole was a man of many secrets.

It began on an innocent evening, a small group of friends answered invitations from a mutual acquaintance of Jerome Tate. By quick observation, Mr. Tate was not easy to describe; ordinary, actually, he was a slender, sickly, pale individual with kinky, reddish-brown hair and an undeveloped goatee. Wire-framed glasses gave him the persona of militancy.

On a college campus or a newsroom, you might take him for a free spirit or a community agitator. But being too overly ripe at thirty-six years of age for a fraternity brother and too nonconformist in attire to work any job, it was safe to classify him as an aging teenager of his generation.

To sustain the lifestyle of a Peter Pan, however, there must be some enabling forces at work. Usually, an overprotective parent with a converted basement for him to live in is a great start. And of course a few social, mental, or physical disabilities that can keep you securely snug in the confines of your launchpad until a plan develops are a must.

Jerome Tate had no problem sharing time and government money with Felix X. Cole where he was being treated for several sketchy mental health issues. This is how Jerome Tate's resume might have looked if he were ever to apply for a job:

> Recovering alcoholic + Recovering drug user + Emotional and anger management problems = Peter Pan Syndrome, with Tinkerbelle playfully "boinging" in his head.

Jerome Tate started a newsletter called "The Happy-Go-Lucky Lollygaggers," An event calendar of sorts that encouraged aging teenagers to meet, greet, and commiserate about the adult world and all its problems. What started as a supper club of like-minded individuals sharing a benign exchange of thoughts and ideas soon became a family of lost souls that found themselves through Cole's bizarre lectures, tabloid film footage, and junk food. They paid membership in the form of dues, and everyone had the same things in common. They idolized Felix X. Cole and the antiestablishment philosophy he espoused.

Jerome Tate began seeing a young woman who was fourteen years younger than he was.

Trinity Dexter was the daughter of posthippie parents. She was a runaway, rescued from a cult group just before her seventeenth birthday and was seeing Dr. Cole for many issues—reprogramming into the real world was one of them. Trinity was responsible for coining the pen name Beanie Boy to Jerome Tate after they became socially engaged. There was no significant reasoning as to why she called Jerome Beanie Boy; when asked later on by followers of the HGLL what Beanie Boy was all about, she would become belligerent and scornful. Trinity was overheard snapping at one member who inquired about the nickname.

"Oh my god, can't anyone just like something because it has a nice ring to it without it meaning something!" she said, almost screaming. "Why does everything have to mean something?"

She began ranting in a shrill voice.

"Jerome 'Beanie Boy' Tate! Jerome 'Beanie Boy' Tate! It sounds nice, doesn't it? Jerome 'Beanie Boy' Tate . . ."

Outside the Lyceum Building, the Happy-Go-Lucky Lollygaggers flash mob are chaining themselves to the building while humming the monotone scales of a tune that was masterminded by Jerome "Beanie Boy" Tate. Cole's protégé and paranoid delusional team organizer was so doped up on psychotropic drugs, he sustained three taser jolts from a riot-control official before he was finally subdued. Beanie Boy was heard humming "God Save the Queen" as they hauled him off.

Jay staggers to his feet, watching Cole quake and tremble, holding the fire extinguisher, ready to smash anyone that attempts to come through the door. He motions to Cindy to remain. Jay attempts to assuage Cole by going into negotiator mode, attempting to reach him by calmly speaking in measured notes, hoping to bring what little reasoning ability Cole might have intact up to the surface.

"Felix, put down the fire extinguisher. So far, nothing is wrong. We haven't done anything to hurt anyone. The police just wants to ask questions. No one is going to hurt you. They are concerned with the crowd that is all."

"They won't get in! My patients are blocking the doorway."

"Felix, you told your patients about this?" an astounded Jay replies.

"Yes, the Happy-Go-Lucky Lollygaggers. They are going to help us."

The commotion in the hallway is getting louder; soon they will be rushing through the door. Cindy shrieks, and Jay calms her.

"Felix, if they think you have a weapon, they might shoot us all."

The police are at the door with orderlies.

Cindy grabs on to Jay's arm and whispers, "Oh my god, Jay, what are we going to do?"

"Cindy, go into the bathroom and lock yourself in," Jay says. "Don't come out until this is over. He is nuts, completely bonkers. I don't know the full story, but they are taking him away."

Jay yells to the police that there is no weapon, just a man with a fire extinguisher.

In the blur of a rush, police and orderlies pour into the room, taking Cole down in a matter of seconds.

Cole lies across the floor with his arms folded across his chest looking up at Jay like a frightened child as the orderlies took control of him, securing him. A stretcher was brought up from the ambulance, and he was laid upon its arms and legs, secured. The only thing he could move was his head and eyeballs.

Jay sat down, answering questions from the police, as Cindy quietly popped her head out from the bathroom, stirring some action from the armed officers. They are pushing Cole through the hallway on a strapped gurney, with Jay and Cindy following. Since they have done nothing wrong, they accompanied Cole to the ambulance from St. Gerard's Medical Center.

Felix X. Cole is staring at Jay from the corner of the crowded elevator, tightly secured in his straitjacket. Foaming spittle is forming at the corner of his mouth. He begins to speak in cryptic sentences.

"They are taking me, Jay. It has to be. Don't worry, we are not alone in this. This is the trial—the crucible. I am going to the big house, the happy farm. Do visit, won't you, Jay? I have been to Eden. I have tasted the fruit and seen the temptress. Art is useless, Jay. A real apple is better than a painted one."

As they push Cole's gurney into the wagon, Jay could still hear him ranting. Jay could see that Cole is straining his pathetic head to look for him one last time, his hair hanging in a mangled lump all helter-skelter.

Jay jogs over to the side of the ambulance where a police officer and an emergency medical worker stop him. Jay's eyes well up with tears for his longtime friend.

Cindy is weeping on the sidewalk, making a sign of the cross across her chest, holding a tissue to her nose as she bowed her head in silent prayer.

Jay could hear Cole's outburst one last time before they close the doors.

"Acey Ducey, whose got Culver Bucy?" Cole blurts out.

A peal of eerie, maniacal laughter echoes from the back of the wagon before getting muffled and cut off—the fading rants of a lunatic as the big bad Mariah hauls off down the street.

Imperceptible to us, eternity enters into metered time without ceasing to be eternal. The enormity of forever whittles into the verse of a poem or a greeting card by way of simple type print:

From the journal of F. X. Cole:

I had an empty time as a teenager.
All my summers were long and never-ending.
The world was so big and solid.
Sometimes I wish I were music-making my own time.

I would like to be a theme, from a Saturday morning Television show.

The hopefulness of those catchy jingles...
Adam was supposed to repair the world on the very first day of his creation.
He insisted on the right to eat from every tree.
Now the famished soul of Adam spreads across earth time.
Not repairing, nor healing, just transposing overlapping earth days into the reintegration of the world itself.
In my room, outside my window is a landscape of the time.
They established law.

They selected lives.
The question now is how to become free.
We must take conscientiousness for all our actions.
Can we still afford the luxury of costly illusions?

Three months have passed since that tragic episode.

Jay proposed to Cindy one month after the fiasco, and they have married the old-fashioned way—in front of a priest in a church on a Sunday.

Cindy asked her cousin Denise to be a maid of honor, and Jay asked his barber of twenty years to be his best man. There was very little fanfare, and the reception was a lovely restaurant where the four of them sat, happily getting to know each other.

The honeymoon was more like a long-awaited vacation. They rented a bed-and-breakfast in a snow-laden little town no one has ever heard of.

The hawk of winter gently frosted the windowpanes of sleepy New England bungalows and winter retreats.

The chime of icicles hanging from the branchy maples and oaks brings a pleasant accompaniment to the crackling Yule log burning off its bark.

Jay sat by the hurricane lamp, reading the memoirs from Cole's new book, his manifesto, *Apples from the Garden of Eden*.

Cindy sat sipping tea, gazing at a dimly lit moon through the trees, listening to vinyl records that were stacked in the corner of the room, along with a phonograph. The assortment of music was magical. There were old Western classics to contemporary standards filling the night with the likes of Gene Autry, Cole Porter, and Dizzy Gillespie. They even waltzed to a Mitch Miller Christmas song at midnight. During a quiet lull, Cindy relaxed in an overstuffed recliner.

"Jay, do you think birds ever think about flying to the moon?" Cindy inquired curiously. "I mean, they go from the ground to a tree to a cloud—"

"No," Jay said. "They never think about putting on sexy pajamas, do they?"

Jay leaped from his chair like lightning and in a downtown second was all over Cindy with devilish frenzy. Jay mounted her and was soon driving it home.

Meanwhile back in the trenches, Felix Cole is huddled in a doorway not but two blocks from the bookshop, The Backward Scholar. He is carefully watching as the crowd begins to swell. Since his release from Gerard Medical Center, Cole has become quite a controversial figure and a new man. The public curiosity about his new book, *Apples from the Garden of Eden*, is exploding and quickly becoming a new cult classic with the university crowd.

On campuses, a matrimonial counterrevolution—an organization called the Happy-Go-Lucky Lollygaggers, now includes tens of thousands of school-age students and is creating a youthquake. Older folks are joining the ranks of a new trend that is sweeping the colleges and soon shaking the core of the age-old institution of marriage across the nation. Students are handing out mock leases and establishing escrow accounts, explaining how couples of all kinds could lease marriages. The theories espoused are from a controversial new book called *Apples from the Garden of Eden* by Dr. Felix Xavier Cole.

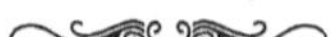

The film file coliseum network ICU broadcast system:

Power play with Dean Topi Presents: The Garden of Eden, Revisited—Dean Topi shares some insight into the working mind of Felix X. Cole and his new book, *Apples from the Garden of Eden.*

Two months ago, a documentary film crew began interviewing Cole at Gerard Medical while he was under observation for an episode of schizophrenic paranoia. What originally was supposed to be a community piece about professional lunacy and an attack on the police turned into a media frenzy when Cole began to address the public with his New Age–style philosophy and mind-changing theories Dr. Cole quoted before a full television audience. Tonight we have some insights on the man Felix X. Cole and his thoughts on art, marriage, and culture.

"We can see the push and pull of religion and man-made law along with mental structures determining personal and cultural conditioning," Dr. Cole says. "Art is dead. We no longer need to react from stimuli from within or without. We must reinvest in our true nature that which is joyous and free from anxiety and limitation. We do not need to drown in technological images we are the image. The only garden we will ever encounter is the Elysian fields we have cultivated."

The crowd went wild. Some say he went too far. Others think an idea whose time has come. What do you think? We will be taking calls 555-800-555 . . .

A tired Felix. X. Cole is resting comfortably on the institutional-style bed and answering fan mail. Every day new piles of letters are flooding the small room at the St. Gerard's psycho ward. He has been recommitted and under further evaluation for violating parole after leading a small group of Happy-Go-Lucky Lollygaggers in a sit-in that resulted in disrupting traffic and causing safety issues in front of The Backward Scholar bookshop where he was invited to do book signings.

According to some, Cole lay prostrate on the street while a circle of Lollygaggers encircled him, chanting, "No fuss, no muss—bring your nuptials to us."

9 781955 156080